LT-M Ferrars
Ferrars, Elizabeth, 1907-
Last will and testament /
Thorndike Press,
2003, c1978.

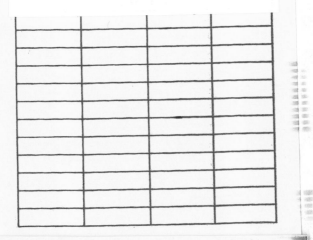

LAST WILL AND TESTAMENT

LAST WILL AND TESTAMENT

Elizabeth Ferrars

CHIVERS
THORNDIKE

This Large Print edition is published by BBC Audiobooks Ltd, Bath, England and by Thorndike Press®, Waterville, Maine, USA.

Published in 2003 in the U.K. by arrangement with the author's estate.

Published in 2003 in the U.S. by arrangement with Harold Ober Associates Inc.

U.K. Hardcover ISBN 0–7540–7376–9 (Chivers Large Print)
U.K. Softcover ISBN 0–7540–7377–7 (Camden Large Print)
U.S. Softcover ISBN 0–7862–5787–3 (Nightingale)

The text of this Large Print edition is unabridged.
Other aspects of the book may vary from the original edition.

Set in 16 pt. New Times Roman.

Printed in Great Britain on acid-free paper.

British Library Cataloguing in Publication Data available

Library of Congress Cataloging-in-Publication Data

Ferrars, Elizabeth, 1907–
        Last will and testament / Elizabeth Ferrars.
        p.   cm.
        ISBN 0–7862–5787–3 (lg. print : sc : alk. paper)
        1. Women physical therapists—Fiction. 2. Divorced Women—
Fiction. 3. Thieves—Fiction. 4. England—Fiction. 5. Large type
books. I. Title.
PR6003.R458L37 2003
823'.912—dc21   2003053355

LT-M

CHAPTER ONE

It was a few minutes after eight o'clock on a fine May morning when I slid my key into the lock of my house in Ellsworthy Street, pushed the door open and knew at once that something was wrong. I could smell cigarette smoke and I had not smoked for ten years.

Walking into the house, I shut the door behind me with some noisiness, hung my coat on a hook in the hall and went into the living-room.

'Of course, it's you,' I said. 'What d'you suppose you're doing here?'

My one-time husband, Felix Freer, got up from the sofa where he had been lying comfortably stretched out and gave me one of his more sheepish smiles.

'If it comes to that, Virginia, where have you been all night?' he asked. 'I've been worried as hell about you.'

'When did you get here?' I demanded.

'About ten o'clock last night.'

'What brought you?'

'For God's sake, why d'you have to use that tone to me?' He stubbed his cigarette out. 'I'd some business in the neighbourhood and thought I'd drop in on you for a chat, that's all. And when you didn't come home and I saw that you didn't seem to have taken anything

1

away with you, not even your toothbrush, I thought I'd better stay on to see if something was wrong.'

'I might have bought myself a new toothbrush,' I said. 'I sometimes do.'

'All right, all right,' he said. 'But with the car gone, you could have been in an accident. I'd made up my mind that if you didn't show up by nine o'clock this morning I'd start phoning the hospitals and possibly the police. Terrible things happen to people, one has to remember that. Sometimes they just disappear and are never heard of again. You'd hardly expect me to leave before I found out, would you?'

'That'll be the day, when you ring the police for help,' I said.

I dropped into a chair. I was too tired to feel much of the helpless, dull anger that I usually did whenever I saw Felix. We had been separated for five years, but I had never been able to get over the bitterness left behind by the brief experience of our marriage.

We had married when we were both thirty-three and had parted three years later. We had never troubled about divorce, but had simply gone our separate ways, Felix continuing his shady, secretive life in London and I returning to the house that I had inherited from my mother in the small town of Allingford, where I had grown up and where I resumed my old part-time practice as a physiotherapist.

I had no real need to work. My mother had

left me enough to live on, if not very lavishly, but I had gone back to the clinic because I preferred it to good works, golf or bridge, while exactly what Felix was doing was something that I preferred not to know too much about.

'How did you get in?' I asked. 'I left the door locked.'

'I've some keys that open most things,' he answered, 'and your lock's particularly easy. You ought to get it changed.'

'I shall,' I said. 'I don't like the feeling that people can drop in here whenever I happen to be out.'

'I'm not just people, surely,' he said. 'We haven't come to that, have we? And suppose something awful had happened to you last night, wouldn't it have been a good thing that I was here?'

'You wouldn't have been here if there'd been any real need for you.'

'That's hardly fair.'

'I know it isn't, but I never want to be fair when I talk to you. It's an effect you have on me.'

'Anyway, where were you last night?'

He had sat down again on the sofa and lit another cigarette. A saucer, which he had been using as an ashtray and which was on the floor near him, was filled to the brim. Assuming that he had not got up very early that morning and had started smoking at once, it looked as if

3

he might really have been enough concerned about me to wait up for quite a long time the night before.

The saucer and the dented cushions and a book that lay open on a chair, where I had left it the afternoon before when the telephone had rung and I had gone at once, gave the room an unkempt, uncared for, early morning look. I always thought it a pleasant room in an undistinguished, late Victorian way, with furniture of several periods that somehow did not quarrel with each other, some pictures that were nothing special, but that I liked, a number of comfortable chairs and a bay window at one end, overlooking my small garden, which was bright just now with lilacs.

Felix smoked nervously and fast, puffing smoke at me as if he needed some kind of screen between us. He sat with his knees apart and his elbows resting on them. I noticed for the first time that there were threads of grey in his fair hair. Yet he was wearing, I felt, far better than I was. At forty-one he was as good-looking as he had been when we married, perhaps even more so. Boyish charm, which had lasted him well into his thirties, was yielding now to an air of distinction. He would soon be able to call himself Professor Sir Felix Freer, or perhaps tell people that he held an important post at the Ministry of Defence, where he worked on matters so secret that they could not fail to be impressed, or that he

4

was a merchant banker who just happened, most unfortunately, to have left his wallet at home.

He was of medium height and slender, with an almost triangular face, wide at the temples, pointed at the chin, with curiously drooping eyelids that made his vivid blue eyes look almost triangular too. He had thick, golden eyebrows and a wide, most friendly mouth. His mouth was not deceptive. In his own fashion he was a most friendly man. He always dressed conservatively and well, though just casually enough to put people at their ease. There were very few people whom Felix could not put at their ease when he chose.

'If you want to know,' I said, 'Mrs Arliss died a few hours ago. They sent for me yesterday afternoon and I've been there ever since. I came home to have a bath and change, then I'll have to go back. There's no one there but her secretary, a nice girl, but she's only twenty-two, and the housekeeper and the chauffeur.'

'Mrs Arliss?' Felix said. 'So she's gone at last. I'm terribly sorry. I know it'll hit you hard. You were really fond of her, weren't you?'

'I suppose so.'

In fact, so far, I was feeling hardly anything at all except exhaustion and an almost pathological craving for a bath. I felt dishevelled and soiled. My skin felt caked with old make-up. My eyes felt as if someone had

5

used his thumbs to push them deep into my head. They smarted as if they had grit in them.

'Why aren't any of the family there?' Felix asked.

'It came as a surprise at the end,' I said. I let my eyes close for a moment, but feeling that if I yielded to the temptation I should fall asleep where I was, I forced them open again. 'She had a stroke three weeks ago and Imogen and Nigel came down. Then she seemed to rally wonderfully. Her left side was a bit paralysed and her speech was a bit slurred, but her mind was absolutely normal and she seemed to be getting better, so they both went home. After all, she might have lingered on literally for years. People sometimes do. And they couldn't hang about indefinitely. And Mrs Bodwell, the housekeeper, is marvellously efficient, and the secretary too, in her way— Meg Randall. Mrs Arliss was very fond of her. She liked having someone young around. Then suddenly yesterday afternoon she had another stroke and never recovered consciousness. She died about five o'clock this morning.'

'You having been sent for by this Meg Randall instead of any of the family,' Felix said. 'I wonder why that was.'

'Simply that I was nearest. I could get to the house in ten minutes. If Imogen or Nigel had been sent for Mrs Arliss might have died long before they got here. Which reminds me, I

6

must telephone them both. Meg left that to me.'

'You mean they don't know yet the old woman's gone?'

'No, there seemed to be so much else to think about and in a way, since she was dead, it didn't seem—well, important.'

'They'll think it a lot more important now than a mere stroke. They'll be down here like a flash. How did she leave her money, do you know?'

I shook my head. 'I don't think they do either. You remember how she was always changing her will, or talking of changing it. I'm not sure if she really got around to doing it. I think she may just have talked about it to scare them. It gave her a nice sense of power.'

'Perhaps there'll be something for you,' Felix suggested.

'No,' I said, 'she told me she wasn't going to leave me anything because money ought to stay in the family and apart from that, she was sure you'd get it out of me. She told me that when she gave me Mary's jewellery, which you may remember, because you pawned it when I wasn't looking. It cost me quite a lot to get it back . . .' I stopped, starting forward in my chair. 'That isn't what you came for! You haven't helped yourself to it again!'

His wide mouth curved downwards, aggrieved.

'As if I'd do a thing like that. Last time I

7

was—well, in certain difficulties and I knew you wouldn't really mind if I'd been able to tell you more about the position I was in.'

'There was nothing to stop you telling me everything, so far as I know, and I minded very much.'

I had indeed. Less because the jewellery was moderately valuable than because Mary Arliss had been my closest friend ever since the two of us, at the age of eleven, had met on our first day at school. Mary had been the only child of the Arliss couple, born when her mother was forty and her father over fifty. He had died only two years later and Mary had become the whole world to her mother. It had been a loving but narrow and stifling world for a child and school had been a wondrous escape for her and the friends that she had made there had all been of extreme importance to her. I had been the one whom she had seemed to care for most. She had taken me to her home where at first I had been only very cautiously welcomed by Mrs Arliss, since I might, after all, be a rival for Mary's affections. But when, at the age of twenty, Mary had died of meningitis, Mrs Arliss had turned to me as the nearest thing to a substitute for her daughter that she had been able to find, and as she grew older she seemed to have become far more attached to me than she had ever been to her niece, Imogen Dale, or her husband's nephew, Nigel Tustin. Mary's jewellery, on one of my birthdays, had been an impulsive gift, expressing a great deal of love. And Felix, within days, had pawned the lot . . .

I stood up, muttering that I must have a bath now, and leaving him, I went upstairs to my room and went straight to the drawer in my dressing-table where I kept my jewel-case.

My suspicions of him had been unjust. Nothing was missing.

Furthermore, there was something on my dressing-table which had not been there when I left the house the day before, a bottle of Estée Lauder's *Alliage.* Looking at it, I gave a resigned sigh, then a slight laugh, shook my head and wearily began to strip off my clothing.

In the hot bath the tension of the night gradually went out of me and I began to feel grief, but only of an almost dreamy, quiet kind that was curiously detached from the inert figure with the yellow-grey face that I had left behind on the bed in the huge bedroom in the Arliss house. The night that I had spent watching Evelyn Arliss die seemed remote, hazy, hard to believe in. Was it the truth, I wondered, that at the time of death it was always hard to believe in it? There were so many things that had to be done, distracting things like those telephone calls that I had promised to make and which must not be put off for too long. Perhaps death only became real at a slight distance.

Getting out of the bath and reaching for a towel, I became aware of a smell of coffee and frying bacon. That was nice. Felix had always made good coffee and I felt ready for a breakfast of bacon and eggs, although normally I began the day with a single slice of toast. Dressing slowly, I put on a green linen skirt and a lighter green blouse and added some ivory beads of Mary's, which I did on an impulse of affection for Mrs Arliss, a small gesture made to please her departed spirit, wherever, if anywhere, it might be. Then I brushed my hair hard, picked up the bottle of *Alliage* and went downstairs.

Felix was in the kitchen, laying the table for two. I put the bottle of scent down on the table before him.

'Thank you, no,' I said.

He looked at me with dismay.

'But I thought it's a kind you like,' he said. 'I chose it on purpose.'

'Of course I like it,' I said, 'but I prefer presents that have been paid for.'

'I know you do,' he said, as if he were making allowances for an eccentricity of mine, 'so I did pay for it.'

'That seems unlikely,' I said.

'It's true, I really did.'

'You don't convince me.'

He turned back to the frying-pan into which he had just broken four eggs.

'I wish I could understand,' he said, 'why I

always find it so difficult to get you to believe me.'

'Because, of course, you so often tell lies.'

I sat down at the table. It had been one of the first disturbing discoveries for me in our marriage that Felix was a dedicated and expert shop-lifter. It had taken me a little while to become convinced of it. At first I had merely found it puzzling that whenever we went out shopping together we nearly always arrived home with more things than I could remember having bought. The unexpected items were often presents for me and usually costly. But I had still been very much in love with him and in a way I was rather shy of him and for a little while I had managed to make myself believe that there was something quite touching about his secretive way of buying these things for me. But they were always unwrapped, which was curious, and one day I had actually seen him pop a lipstick into his pocket while I had been buying some nail varnish. Later, with a loving kiss, he had given me the lipstick and I had tried to make myself challenge him about it, but I had not had the courage and for some time after that I had said nothing about this deplorable habit of his, trying to think of how I could help to cure him of it. For of course I had been sure that it was simply kleptomania, which was an illness and not in any real sense criminal. But going out with him had turned into a terrifying experience, as day by day I

11

waited for him to be caught, while accepting his presents had made me feel like a receiver of stolen property, which was just what I was, after all.

At last, without quite realizing what I was going to do, I had suddenly turned on him and told him what I knew about him and he had blandly denied everything.

I had known by then how many lies he told, which I had been almost able to tolerate, telling myself that he lived in a world of fantasy and that I could help him to grow out of it. But his lying then seemed to mean that he took me for an absolute fool. We had had a terrible quarrel, which had ended most horribly with his bursting into tears, saying that I was the only hope he had of ever going straight, in the middle of which I had seen, I was sure, a gleam of laughter in his eyes. That was when I had revised my opinion of his kleptomania and had begun to ask myself questions about certain other ways he had. About how he earned his money, for instance. He had told me that he was a civil engineer and told me the name of the firm that he worked for and it had never occurred to me to check up on this. But when I did it turned out that they had never heard of him. I had finally discovered that he worked for a dubious firm of second-hand car dealers, whose managing director happened to be in gaol for fraud.

Felix put the coffee-pot down on the table

and turned back to the frying-pan.

'I bought that stuff for you at Fortnum's,' he said, 'and I paid good cash for it. But throw it back in my face if you want to.'

I poured out a cup of coffee.

'Even if you did, I wonder what other little luxuries you came away with,' I said. I sipped the coffee. 'This is very good. Perhaps it'll put some stiffening back into me. I need it.'

'You look worn out,' Felix said. 'Have you really got to go back to that place? What you need is some sleep.'

'I'm afraid I've got to go. I'll pull myself together presently.'

He slid the eggs out of the pan on to two plates that had rashers of bacon on them and put one of the plates down in front of me.

'That ought to help,' he said. 'Now listen. I did pay for that scent, I swear I did, and I did that just to please you. So why can't you accept it in that spirit?'

He spoke in a tone of earnest sincerity. As he sat down facing me and poured coffee into his own cup, his eyes were candid and clear and full of concern for me. The concern at least was probably genuine. He was easily moved to sympathy with others, though he seldom remembered to go on feeling it for long.

'I just wish you wouldn't bring me presents at all,' I said. I started on the bacon and eggs. 'And, as I've told you before, I don't want you

13

to come here.'

'I just like to see you sometimes to make sure things are going all right with you,' he said.

'It seems to me you just want to keep some kind of hold on me, in case it'll come in useful sometime,' I answered. 'It'll never work, you know. I've told you that before. What's this business you had in the neighbourhood?'

'I was delivering a car to a customer.'

'So you're still in the second-hand car racket.'

He frowned. 'Racket is a nasty word. We're a strictly legitimate business.'

'You mean you aren't buying up old wrecks that have been in smashes and transferring their registrations and so on to stolen cars and doing very nicely out of selling them? I thought that was a much too profitable thing for you ever to give up.'

He shook his head. 'I'm growing wise in my old age. I don't like taking risks any more.'

'I wish I could believe that.'

'You don't, you know. You don't care in the least.'

'Not very much, perhaps, because the truth is I simply don't believe you.'

He sighed. 'Do you know, you've become very hard, Virginia? Almost a shrew. That's bad. It's a thing that'll get worse as you get older, if you aren't careful, do you know that? Perhaps it's living alone. You do live alone, I imagine.'

'Quite alone,' I said. 'Do you?'

'More or less.'

'Still at the old address in Little Carbery Street?'

'Yes, I'm still there. I've got attached to the old place and I could easily pay more and be no better off. You should come along and see it sometime. I've made some improvements, redecorated it—I did most of that myself—got some new curtains and so on. It's really very nice.'

I helped myself to more coffee. It was doing me good. My eyes had lost their gritty feeling and my mind felt clearer. And the bacon and eggs were ridding me of a nervous hunger that I had felt ever since I had arrived home. I felt some gratitude to Felix. He had always been a wonderfully domesticated man, clever at cooking, always ready to be helpful.

I drew the bottle of *Alliage* towards me.

'Well, thank you for this,' I said. 'I'm sorry I was horrid about it.'

He looked genuinely pleased. 'You'll keep it?'

'Yes.'

I did not really mean to keep it. I could easily hand it on as a Christmas present to some unsuspecting person who would have no misgivings about its provenance. But there was nothing to be gained by telling Felix this and hurting him. It would make him neither better

15

nor worse than he was.

'I'll start that telephoning now,' I went on when I had finished my coffee. 'I'll begin with Imogen. She ought just about to be getting up now. Early rising isn't one of her habits, but at least she should be awake. I'll have to ring Nigel at his office, I suppose.' I stood up. 'Thank you for my breakfast. What a treasure of a husband you'd be if only one could trust you.'

I left the kitchen, went back to the living-room, dialled Imogen Dale's number and settled myself in a corner of the sofa for what I thought was likely to turn out a lengthy conversation.

Imogen lived in a small Regency house in Hampstead. She had never married, preferring less binding relationships with men than marriage made convenient. She was very handsome, a tall, robust woman, seething with vigour. She was the daughter of Mrs Arliss's younger sister and was nearly the same age as I was. She had thick, dark hair, a high colour, a straight, arrogant nose and a small, well-shaped mouth. Her dark eyes were wide and shining, but a little blank and it was never easy to guess at what was going on behind them. She had a habit of taking up interests suddenly, as diverse as pony-trekking, silversmithing and Conservative politics, declaring them the one and only object that she would ever have in her life, then dropping

16

them as abruptly as she did her lovers.

Her voice on the telephone, reciting her number, sounded throatily sleepy.

I answered, 'Imogen, it's Virginia. I hope I didn't wake you, but it's something important.'

'Not to worry.' The answer came through a yawn. 'I'm still in bed. I'm quite comfortable. I've a telephone beside me. What is it? Are you coming up to town? Can we have lunch together?'

'No, I'm afraid I've some bad news,' I said. Actually I was not at all sure how bad my news would be to Imogen. She had not had any very convincing affection for her aunt that I had ever noticed. 'Mrs Arliss had another stroke yesterday afternoon and she died early this morning. Dr Wickham came at once when she had the stroke. He said there was no point in moving her into hospital, that there was nothing anyone could do. I was with her when she died. I'd have got in touch with you sooner, only there seemed to be so much to do and you couldn't have helped. I don't think she suffered at all. She never regained consciousness.'

There was silence from the other end of the line, then I heard what sounded like a long breath being let out.

'Poor old thing,' Imogen said. Her voice was awake now, but quite calm. 'In a way it's a blessing, isn't it? I mean, after that first stroke she was never quite herself. And she was so

17

proud and independent, being half-helpless must have distressed her terribly. I'm glad you were with her. We all owe you a great deal for the way you've looked after her these last few years. She was devoted to you. Does Nigel know about this?'

'Not yet. Shall I telephone him, or will you?'

'Will you? That would be such a help. I'll have so much to think about. I ought to come down, I suppose, at least in time for the funeral. When will that be?'

'Naturally nothing's been settled yet.' I wondered what deep thinking Imogen needed to do as a result of her aunt's death. 'It's really for you and Nigel to decide.'

'I'd far sooner leave it to you. You're much better than I am at arranging things and Nigel hates coping with anything that interferes with his normal routine. So be an angel, will you, Virginia, and take charge? But I'll telephone Paul, if you like. I suppose he ought to know.'

Paul Goss was a nephew of Imogen's, Mrs Arliss's only grand-nephew.

'And have you thought of getting in touch with Patrick?' Imogen went on. 'When he knows, perhaps he'll take over all the arrangements.'

Patrick Huddleston had been Mrs Arliss's solicitor, a member of the Allingford firm of Huddleston, Huddleston and Weekes, who had looked after the affairs of Mrs Arliss and her husband for forty years.

18

'Wouldn't it be best for you to get in touch with them?' I said. 'After all, I'm not family. He might wonder why I was taking so much on myself.'

'But you're on the spot. Still, if that's how you feel, I'll telephone him. And I'll come down this afternoon. Can I stay in the house? I suppose that couple, the Bodwells, are still running things. If not, I could go to a hotel.'

'They're running things very competently.' I knew that if there had been the slightest risk that she might have to help in the running of the house, even in a time of crisis, Imogen would have gone straight to a hotel. Not that it mattered. In fact, it might be easiest for everyone if she did that. 'Meg Randall too,' I said. 'Poor girl, I think it's the first time she's had to deal with death. She's very shaken, but she's kept her head very well.'

'Ah yes, Meg. I'd forgotten about her. She won't actually be needed any more, will she? Has she a home to go to, do you know, till she gets another job?'

'I don't know. But don't you think she might stay on for a while? She might be useful to Patrick when it comes to sorting out Mrs Arliss's affairs.'

'I hadn't thought of that. Perhaps. Not that I suppose her affairs are so awfully complicated. Well, thank you for ringing, Virginia, and I'll be down some time this afternoon. I'll find you at the house, shall I?'

19

'I expect so.'

I rang off, waited a moment, then dialled Nigel Tustin's office number.

He was the son of Mr Arliss's one sister and though he had been no blood relation of Mrs Arliss, had always been treated by her as a nephew of her own. She had had a fair amount of affection for him and had treated him with rather more kindliness than she ever had Imogen, whose manner of life she had disapproved of. Yet she had never been able to resist playing Imogen off against him whenever she had felt that he was showing too much interest in how she was going to leave her money. She had always refused to set the minds of the two of them at rest simply by telling them that she would divide it equally between them. At different times one or the other had been the favourite to whom she was going to leave it all. But then the favourite would somehow offend and her will would be changed. How things stood now, which of them was to inherit her fortune, I had no idea. Whatever happened, I thought, there would be bitterness, quarrelling, perhaps even threats of the will being contested, unless Patrick Huddleston managed to control them both very firmly.

Nigel answered my telephone call promptly. He was a member of a firm of architects in Oxford and lived in a small Georgian house, surrounded by Georgian furniture, in a village

20

a few miles out of the town. But he would never have put his name to any design of a house that did not consist of curious, white, box-like shapes, strangely tumbled together and with whole walls of glass. He was fairly prosperous, a rather portly man of fifty-five, always sleekly groomed, with dark hair receding from a high, smooth forehead, long, plump cheeks and a slightly ponderous manner. He was the kind of bachelor who can always keep some elderly widowed housekeeper devotedly attached to him, treating her with great respect and generosity, carefully aimed at maintaining the maximum amount of comfort for himself.

He listened to what I told him about the death of his aunt without interrupting, then said thoughtfully, 'Well, well.'

For a moment I thought that that was all that he was going to say. I could imagine him smoothing his thinning hair back from his forehead.

Then, like Imogen, he remarked, 'A blessing, when all's said and done, though losing her is naturally a shock. Death always comes as a shock, even when one's expecting it. I'm so glad you were with her, Virginia. Thank you for all your kindness. I'm most grateful. I'm sure Imogen is too. I'll drive over and hope to see you this afternoon. Now, unfortunately, I have an appointment that I must keep, though I'm afraid I may find it rather hard to concentrate. Yes, death is decidedly a shock.'

That was all. He rang off. I put the telephone down and looking round, found Felix in the doorway, listening to me.

'A horrible job, having to break bad news,' he remarked. 'Were there agonies of grief?'

'Not exactly,' I said.

'No one will weep at my funeral when I die,' he said. 'No one will care. You, of course, won't even come to it.'

'Do you want me to?' I asked. 'I'd hate to let you down at a time like that.'

'You're invited, of course, but I know you won't put in an appearance. Do you know, it's depressing to feel so sure of that. After all, we had some good times together, didn't we?'

That was a line he sometimes tried that I would never tolerate. I got to my feet.

'Unless you're in a crack-up, driving one of your stolen cars, you're most unlikely to die for quite a long time yet,' I said. 'I may well race you to it. I'm going out now. I don't know when I'll be back. You're going back to London, I suppose.'

'You don't want me to stay here?'

'I don't mind what you do, but there's nothing for you to stay for.'

'Except that I like seeing a little of you now and then. Only you hate me. I always forget, when I'm away from you, how much you hate me. I have to see that certain look in your eyes to remember.'

'I don't really hate you,' I said. 'I've tried to, but it doesn't work. The fact is, you'd make an excellent husband for a very rich woman. You're domesticated, good-tempered, affectionate and if you had a lot of money behind you, you might even really learn to go straight. You might think it was worth your while and you might make the woman very happy.'

'Now there's real hatred in saying a thing like that,' he said. 'All right, I'll be gone when you come back.'

He reached for the coat that I had hung up in the hall and helped me into it. As he did so, he kissed me gently on the back of my neck.

'I did pay for that scent, you know,' he said. 'I'm glad you're going to keep it.'

The worst of it was, he occasionally spoke the truth. So you never knew where you were with him.

CHAPTER TWO

Mrs Arliss had lived in a big house which at the time when it had been built had been in the country, but in the last thirty years had been encircled by the suburbs of Allingford. But it still had the privacy given to it by a big garden and a high beech hedge that screened it from the houses round it. It had a long drive, bordered by rhododendrons which blazed just now with clumps of crimson bloom, a group of tall trees shading a sloping lawn, a complicated rockery and a long, formal herbaceous border.

The garden had been very well looked after for the last year by Jim Bodwell, the husband of Mrs Arliss's highly efficient housekeeper. He had also driven the Rolls and been useful about the house. When I drove in at the gate he was in the garden as usual, hoeing the border.

Seeing me, he straightened up and came towards me. He was a tall, spare man of about fifty with a brown, bony face and pale grey eyes. Opening the door of my car for me, he stood leaning on his hoe. As always, there was an air of rather formidable reserve about him.

'Sad, isn't it?' he said. 'But it comes to us all. I don't know rightly if I should be out here now, just as if nothing had happened, but there's nothing I can do in the house and once

24

let a garden get out of hand, you'll spend months regretting it. It kind of takes your mind off things too, working. They'll be selling the place now, I suppose.'

There was a question in his voice. It occurred to me that the most important thing that the death of Mrs Arliss meant to him and his wife would undoubtedly be the loss of their jobs.

'I don't know,' I answered. 'Miss Dale and Mr Tustin will be here this afternoon. I don't expect they'll decide anything in a hurry.'

'But they won't keep this house on, will they? They've both got homes of their own and a place like this isn't everyone's cup of tea. Too big and old-fashioned for most people nowadays, though the wife and I have been happy here. But likely as not it'll be turned into flats now, or an old folks' home, or some such thing, and we shan't be wanted by the new people, whoever they are.'

'You won't find any difficulty in getting another job,' I said. 'A good gardener and a good housekeeper are worth their weight—in gold. And I know you'll be given splendid references.'

'That's something I was wondering about,' he said. 'Who'll give them to us now that Mrs Arliss has passed away? Miss Dale, would you say? Or Mr Tustin? They don't really know us very well, either of them.'

'They both knew what Mrs Arliss thought of

25

you and that'll be good enough for them. You've nothing whatever to worry about.'

I turned towards the house. It was built of dark red brick, of the unlovely kind that never weathers, with dark green ivy patchily covering the walls. There were small turrets at the corners of the roof and rows of tall, blind-looking sash windows. It was a charmless building that had tried to be imposing and failed.

The front door was standing open when I went up the steps to it and Meg Randall was in the doorway.

'I saw you arrive,' she said. 'I'm so glad you've come back. I—I don't much like being on my own here. Silly of me, but I can't help it.'

She was pale and very tense. She was at all times pallid, yet usually there was a look of health in her clear skin and grave blue eyes that gave them a kind of glow. But this had vanished during the demanding hours of the night. She was small, slender and rather fragile-looking, with fair hair that hung straight to her shoulders, and she was still wearing what she had worn all night, a blue shirt, matching jeans and sandals.

'But you aren't alone here,' I said as I took off my coat. 'There's Mrs Bodwell.'

'Yes, but I can't talk to her,' Meg replied. 'She's disappeared into the kitchen and except that she brought me some breakfast, she seems

26

to want to be left to herself. Of course, she never does talk much. Mrs Arliss said that was one of the excellent things about her, that she didn't want a daily session of gossip as part of her wages. But ever since you and Dr Wickham left there's been such a silence in the house that I've been—oh, I may as well admit it—scared. I've been telling myself how stupid that is, but it makes no difference.'

'I think the Bodwells are worrying about what's going to happen to them,' I said. 'But of course a couple like them will get another job immediately.'

'I wonder what will happen to me,' Meg said.

She turned towards the door of the small morning-room which Mrs Arliss had used far more than the big, formal drawing-room. I followed her, stepping through pools of bright colour on the polished tiles of the floor, which fell on them through the panes of stained glass in a window half way up the stairs.

Sitting down on one of the low, velvet-covered chairs where Mrs Arliss had liked to sit, working at her embroidery, I saw some of this embroidery, a piece of patchwork, with a gold thimble and a pair of spectacles, still on a table under the window. What did you do with things like that, I wondered. Clothes you could send to a Thrift Shop. Furniture you could sell. But an unfinished piece of embroidery? Did you just throw it away? That seemed heartless.

'You haven't got to decide all at once,' I said, 'unless you're in a hurry to leave. Are you?'

Meg had thrown herself down on a neat little Victorian sofa, where her young, sprawling limbs looked very incongruous against its prim prettiness.

'I don't know what I want to do,' she said. 'It doesn't seem right to be thinking about oneself at a time like this, yet somehow one can't help it. I never meant to stay on as long as I did, you know. I mean, I could see at once it was just a dead end job. Very easy, of course, and well paid and Mrs Arliss was very good to me and I got quite fond of her. But still it could be pretty boring and it wasn't getting me anywhere and I kept making up my mind I ought to leave and start looking for something with better prospects. Then Mrs Arliss would say something that would suddenly make me feel she really depended on me and that it would be horribly unkind to leave her. After all, she never cared much for those relations of hers, did she, or they for her? She had you and me and really nobody else. Sometimes I got the feeling I knew far more about her than anybody else, even you. Did you know about her gambling, for instance?'

The look I gave her must have been one of complete astonishment.

'Gambling?' I exclaimed. 'Mrs Arliss?'

Meg nodded vehemently, so that her fair

28

hair swung about her shoulders.

'Oh yes. Horses. I used to have to place her bets for her. And I had to promise I'd never tell anyone. She said if her family found out, they'd be sure she was getting senile and try to get a power of attorney, so that she couldn't touch her own money. And it was her one real interest in life, you know.'

'Did she mostly win or lose?' I asked.

'I think she broke about even,' Meg answered. 'She used to bet quite large sums and I suppose on the whole she lost a bit more than she won, but there wasn't much in it, and as I said, it was her one real pleasure.'

'I wonder why I wasn't let into the secret.' I was surprised at how much I was hurt by the discovery of how little I had been in Mrs Arliss's confidence.

'She said you'd worry, just as you used to worry about your husband.' Meg gave a great yawn, turning her head to bury her face in a cushion. 'Oh God, I'm tired,' she mumbled into it. 'I don't think I've ever felt so tired in my life.' Then she turned her head and looked up at me again. 'Nobody ever talks about your husband,' she said. 'What's the matter with him?'

'Well, in some ways he's a difficult person to live with.'

'You know, a sort of hush falls on people if one mentions him—'

The telephone rang.

29

Meg jerked up sharply on the sofa. She was accustomed to answering the telephone in this house. She gave Mrs Arliss's number, then said, 'Mrs Freer's here. Perhaps you'd better speak to her.' Then she held the telephone out to me.

I got up and took it from her.

'Yes?' I said.

'Virginia? This is Patrick,' said the pleasant tenor voice of Patrick Huddleston. 'I've just heard from Imogen that Mrs Arliss died in the night. I rang up to find out if there's anything I can do.'

'I don't know,' I said. 'I don't really know what needs to be done. Dr Wickham said he'd get in touch with the undertakers for us and I suppose they'll—well, take over. I'm just staying here till Imogen and Nigel arrive. They've both said they'll come here this afternoon.'

'This afternoon? Perhaps that's when I should come then. Unless I can help in any way now. Are you sure there's nothing I can do?'

'Is there anything to be done but wait?'

'I suppose not, but if you think of anything . . .' He paused. 'Mrs Arliss was an old friend— that's to say, really a friend of my father's— and I'd like to help in any way I can. If you want me, I'll be in the office for the rest of the morning, then I'll come over in the afternoon.'

'Thank you.'

'How's Meg managing?'

'Pretty well, considering.'

'She's so very young. I'm glad she isn't alone there, though of course there are the Bodwells. Good, reliable people in a crisis, I should say. Well, don't hesitate to call me if you want me for anything.'

He rang off.

I sat down again.

'Have you any family you can go to for the time being?' I asked Meg.

'My parents live in Devon,' she replied, 'and I could always go back to them, but I don't think I will. We don't get on too well. They still treat me as if I need a sitter-in if they go out in the evenings. But I've got some money saved up, so I haven't got to rush things. I expect I'll go to London and look for a job there. Something in an office, with a lot of people in it. I'd like that for a change. On the other hand, I don't know, I might even look for something in Allingford. I've quite a number of friends here and Mr Huddleston said something once about their wanting someone in their office. Of course, he may not have meant it, but it would be interesting, I should think, working in a lawyer's office. Mrs Arliss liked him very much, you know. She said he was very human for a solicitor.'

'All the same, she didn't let him know about her betting, did she?'

Meg frowned uneasily. 'I don't think I ought

31

to have said anything about that. I wish I hadn't.'

The door opened and Mrs Bodwell came in.

She was a tall, quiet-looking woman of about the same age as her husband, with hair that was of the steely-grey that had probably once been black and with large, sombre eyes in a fine-boned, colourless face. She was wearing black, but this was not mourning for Mrs Arliss, for I had never seen her in anything else. She was carrying a tray with cups and a teapot on it.

'I made you some tea, Mrs Freer,' she said in her low, flat voice. 'I thought you and Miss Randall could do with it. Will you be staying for lunch?'

'Will it be a trouble if I do?' I asked. 'Miss Randall and I could go out if it would make things easier for you.'

'It's no trouble at all.' Mrs Bodwell put the tray down on a table. 'I'd like to know, though, are any of the family expected? There's food in the freezer, so that's no problem, but if they're staying the night, I thought I'd start getting their rooms ready for them.'

'Miss Dale and Mr Tustin are arriving this afternoon,' I said, 'and will probably be staying the night if you can manage.'

I knew that Mrs Bodwell would manage perfectly. Except for some help from her husband and from a woman who came in two mornings a week, she had run the big house

32

single-handed for the last year and had never been known to complain that anything was too much for her.

'I'll come and help, shall I?' I added.

'Perhaps with the beds, if you'd care to have something to do,' Mrs Bodwell said. 'Do you think Miss Dale and Mr Tustin will be staying long?'

'I suppose until after the funeral,' I said.

'And I don't suppose it's decided yet when that's to be.'

'In three or four days, I imagine.'

She nodded thoughtfully. 'Then Jim and I will have to look for a new place to go to. We'll be sorry to leave here. It's suited us nicely. And we don't want to inconvenience anybody, but we've got to think of ourselves and the sooner we get fixed up, the better.'

'Perhaps Miss Dale and Mr Tustin will ask you to stay on till the house is sold,' I said. 'It puts people off if a place doesn't look cared for and you've looked after it so well.'

'I don't think we'd really care to stay now that poor Mrs Arliss has passed on,' Mrs Bodwell answered. 'It would be a big responsibility, looking after the place by ourselves.'

I looked at her curiously, wondering if there was really something as strange as I felt there was about the impatience of the Bodwells to leave the house, or if it was natural for people like them, who had no home of their own, perhaps no savings and some fear of the future, to feel more distrust of the class of employers than they had ever allowed to appear before.

I repeated what I had said to her husband. 'You'll get a new job at once.'

'It's just we like to know where we are,' she said. She looked out of the window. 'Here are the undertaker's men,' she said in her toneless voice, 'come to measure the body. Will it be a burial or a cremation, d'you know? I've a feeling Mrs Arliss would prefer to be buried.'

I had poured out the tea and handed a cup to Meg, but now I put mine down, thinking that it was I who would have to take the undertaker's men up to the darkened bedroom where the dead woman lay in icy solitude.

'Unless she's left instructions in her will, it's a matter for the family to decide,' I said and went to meet the two men whose car was at the front door and who had just come up to it, greeting me, when I appeared, with solemn courtesy. They introduced themselves as Mr Robertson and Mr Jarvis, Funeral Directors, and asked to be allowed to view the deceased.

The deceased, I thought. The body. The remains. No longer Mrs Arliss, but only what, to be honest, had become a considerable inconvenience to a number of people, to be shuffled out of the way as expeditiously as possible.

The next visitor to arrive at the house was

the Reverend Matthew Bailey, vicar of St Hilary's, the church that Mrs Arliss had attended for the last fifty years. She had seen vicars come and vicars go, and Matthew Bailey, a serious young man with a curiously hushed, whispering way of speaking, even when he was in the pulpit, had been in Allingford for only five years. To Mrs Arliss, of whose death he had heard from Dr Wickham, he had been a mere boy, too immature for her to have much regard for him. But in the sad little talk that he and I had about her he showed respect and even affection for the old woman, speaking with feeling of her piety and her charities and of how much she would be missed.

The next visitor, arriving about an hour after the cold lunch that Mrs Bodwell served up for Meg and me, was Patrick Huddleston.

He arrived in a new white Rover and emerged from it looking almost as festive as if he were on his way to a wedding. But that was how he always looked. Slim, gracefully built, dressed usually in pale grey with exuberantly coloured shirts and appearing much younger than his age, which I knew was thirty-seven, he had an irrepressible air of cheerfulness, which, it struck me now, must often be as out of place in a solicitor's office as it was at the present moment. He came into the house smiling. However, the smile seemed to be one mainly of kindliness and sympathy and at least he was wearing a plain white shirt instead of one of the flowered ones that he favoured. He had curly dark hair, which he wore rather long, skin which was naturally dark as well as being tanned by the hours that he spent on the golf course, and long-lashed dark eyes in a narrow, nervous face.

Seeing Meg, he put an arm round her and held her briefly to him, brushing one of her temples with a kiss. It was only the conventional kiss of greeting, but from the way that Meg flushed a deep red, I thought that it meant more to her than he could have intended. Then a sullen look settled on her face, as if she were trying to erase the effect of that moment of self-betrayal.

Patrick put a hand on my shoulder and gave it a gentle pressure.

'This is terrible, isn't it?' he said. 'Aren't the others here yet?'

'No.' I led the way towards the drawing-room. It seemed to me the right place for the family to meet and discuss what they must with Mrs Arliss's solicitor. The little room where Meg and I had sat before lunch was too small to hold us all. 'I'll stay till they come, but then I'll go home. There's nothing now I can do here.'

'I'm sure they'll want you to stay,' he said. 'Can you see either of them wanting to take any responsibility? Though perhaps that's hard on you. You've done enough already and you must be very tired. By the way, I've sent notices of Mrs Arliss's death to *The Times* and the *Allingford Echo,* and said that the funeral will be at St Hilary's the day after tomorrow. No flowers by request. I've just fixed it up with the vicar. I hope it was the right thing to do. I don't know if it will suit Imogen and Nigel, but I thought they'd probably be glad to have the whole thing settled for them.'

'I'm sure they will.'

The big room felt cold although the sun was shining in at the windows. But this room had always felt cold, as long as I could remember. It had a very high ceiling with an ornate plaster cornice and an immense crystal chandelier hanging from its centre. The furniture was mostly of dark mahogany and the chairs were covered in shiny silk, which looked as if no one had ever sat on it. There were portraits of Mr and Mrs Arliss in their youth, very indifferently painted, in oval frames hanging over the marble fireplace. A collection of miniatures made long ago by Mr Arliss and treasured for his sake by Mrs Arliss decorated one wall. A tall french window opened on to a terrace, edged with a low stone balustrade. Wanting to let some of the warmth from the garden into the room, I went to this window and opened it wide.

Patrick came to my side.

'This room is really a period piece, isn't it?' he said. 'With the present fashion for

Victorian, the stuff in it should be fairly valuable.'

'I think it's mostly reproduction and not really worth much,' I answered.

'But at least the house should fetch a good deal. Lucky Imogen.'

'Then she's inherited it in the end, has she?'

'Except for a few things. Not that I've checked up yet, but that's what I remember of the last will I had to draw up.'

'That'll be a blow for Nigel.'

'Oh, he's all right. He's doing very nicely, becoming quite well known. And he hasn't got extravagant habits, like Imogen.'

'But—' Meg said suddenly and loudly, then stopped herself as abruptly as she had interrupted.

Patrick and I both turned to look at her. She was standing with her back to the empty fireplace and again a flush had spread over her pallid face. She stared at us both as if she were afraid of us, then sharply turned her back, gripping the mantelpiece with both hands and staring up, apparently with intense concentration, at the portraits of the young Mr and Mrs Arliss.

'Something wrong, Meg?' Patrick asked.

'No,' she answered in a low voice.

'If you think it's a bit indecent to be talking of such things so soon after Mrs Arliss's death, I think you're quite right,' he said. 'But it's a thing people do.'

'But the fact is—' she began, then stopped again.

'Yes?'

He could sound so gentle and full of understanding that I really did not feel surprised that Meg, as I thought was the case, had been strongly attracted by him.

'Oh, you're so *stupid*!' she exclaimed. 'You're her solicitor and you don't even know . . .'

Then she swung round and darted out of the room.

Patrick raised an eyebrow at me. 'What was all that about, d'you think?'

'I've a feeling that it's connected somehow with the fact that Mrs Arliss took to gambling in a fairly big way in recent times,' I said. 'Did you know about that?'

His dark eyes widened. 'Good God, no! Are you serious?'

'I think Meg was serious when she told me.'

'What kind of gambling?'

'Horses. She kept it very secret from the family in case they should think that at her age it meant she was going mad. And if you're going to ask me did she lose a great deal and is that what's on Meg's mind, she told me that Mrs Arliss broke about even, or only lost a little.'

He gave a quiet laugh. 'Horses, at her time of life! What a remarkable old woman she was in her way, wasn't she? I hope she got some pleasure out of it. But I'd like to know what I've done that Meg thinks is so stupid.'

The doorbell rang. The firm footsteps of Mrs Bodwell crossed the hall as she went to answer it. A moment later Nigel Tustin came into the drawing-room.

He was wearing an excellently cut, double-breasted dark suit, perfectly pressed, a white shirt and an obviously new black tie. His long, plump cheeks were a little sallower than usual, but his eyes were calm. Holding out a hand to me in silence, then to Patrick, he planted himself in the middle of the room, looking thoughtfully around him, as if he were experimentally trying it on for fit, to see how he would feel when it belonged to him.

'Good of you both to be here,' he said. 'Isn't Imogen here yet?'

'She's coming sometime, I believe,' I answered.

'And Paul?'

'I don't know.'

'Not that there's anything one can do,' Nigel said. 'Still, one feels a responsibility. The—the arrangements—I imagine they've been taken care of.'

'I've been in touch with the undertaker and the vicar, if that's what you mean,' Patrick said. 'The funeral's fixed for the day after tomorrow.'

'Good of you, very. I appreciate it. There are no problems then?'

40

'Problems? What sort of problems should there be?'

'Oh, I don't know. Amazing, really, at my time of life, how little experience I've had of this sort of thing. The death certificate, for instance. No hitch about that, I suppose.'

'My dear Nigel, she was eighty-three, she had a severe stroke three weeks ago, rallied fairly well, then had another stroke yesterday and died this morning, with Dr Wickham in attendance. There certainly won't be an inquest, if that's what's worrying you.'

'No, no, of course not. I'm sorry, I'm feeling a little confused. Actually, I've been expecting this news about her ever since the first stroke, but now that it's come, it's hard to believe in it. She's always been there, all my life. She seemed so indestructible. A splendid woman. She was very kind to me. Perhaps—what d'you think?—I ought to go up and take a—well, a last look at her.'

'Of course, if you want to,' Patrick said. 'Shall I come up with you?'

'No, I'd just as soon go on my own, just to say goodbye and all that, thank you. It's strange, you know, I saw plenty of death in the war, but that was all violent death, mostly of young men and messy. This is the first time I've seen anyone who died peacefully in her bed. I find it curiously awesome. Well, I shan't be a minute.'

He walked sedately out of the room.

'Why didn't you tell him he's getting nothing and put him out of his misery?' I asked.

'I'm not sure that he doesn't get anything at all,' Patrick answered. 'I ought to have checked it before I came here, but I didn't think there'd be any special hurry about it. I suppose I felt that one ought to let a decent interval elapse before discussing the matter.'

I looked out of the french window that I had opened. There was a white bench on the terrace a few yards away from the window and all at once I felt an intense longing to sit on the bench, surrounded by the freshness and life of the garden, instead of the old age and death that pervaded the house. After hesitating a moment, I stepped out on to the terrace, walked the few yards to the bench and sat down on it.

In a flower-bed near me, full of tulips and forget-me-nots, a female blackbird was tugging at a fat worm, and I found myself thinking what devoted parents birds are, working all day long to feed their ravening young. Then I went on to wonder rather drowsily what Felix and I would have been like if we had happened to have children.

Would children have made any difference to us? But Felix was basically such a child himself that it was almost impossible to imagine him as a father. It had seemed in the end one of the few good things about our marriage that there had been no children to worry about.

But Mrs Arliss would have liked us to have children. The old woman had had an abundance of maternal feeling that had been badly starved after Mary's death. Neither Nigel nor Imogen had been able to satisfy it. I had done my best, but what Mrs Arliss had wanted was someone younger, someone as young as Mary had been, someone as young, I suddenly thought, as Meg Randall . . .

The blackbird sliced the worm up neatly into equal lengths, gathered them up with her beak and flew away.

Was it possible then that Mrs Arliss had changed her will yet once more, without letting Patrick know of it, because of course he would have tried to argue her out of it, and left all her wealth to Meg? Was that what was upsetting the girl, that she knew of it and was scared of having to face the family when they found it out? Scared of them contesting the will, as they almost certainly would, making out that she was an evil, scheming young woman who had made use of her position to bring undue influence to bear on a helpless old woman and so enrich herself immensely?

As perhaps she had . . .

I did not know her at all intimately and I had emerged from my marriage with my capacity for trust sadly damaged. Suspicion proliferated easily in my mind. I was not, I realized, nearly as nice a person as I had been before I met Felix.

The sunshine was warm on my face. The garden was full of bird-song and the scent of wallflowers. My eyes closed.

When I woke presently I did not know how long my sleep had lasted. It might have been only a few minutes, but it seemed to have left me even wearier than I had been before. Rubbing my eyes, getting to my feet, I returned to the open french window.

In the room inside Imogen and Patrick Huddleston were in each other's arms and their kiss was not the conventional kiss of greeting. They were both lost in it, unaware of anything but one another.

Unaware, for sure, of the white-faced girl whom I saw across the room in the doorway to the hall, staring at them with a look of agonized shock on her face.

As I stood there, hesitating, Meg turned quickly and vanished from the room. After an instant I also turned away. Sitting down again on the bench for a minute or two, I got up once more, made a slightly absurd pantomime of coughing as I returned to the french window and went in.

Imogen and Patrick were on opposite sides of the fireplace, both sitting down, but there was a faintly mocking look on Imogen's face, as if she knew quite well what all that coughing had meant. There was a sardonic look in her dark eyes. She was in a plain grey flannel suit, more restrained than she usually wore and somewhat out of date, as if she had brought it out of retirement for the occasion.

'Hallo, Virginia,' she said. 'Patrick's been telling me how much you've helped. Of course I'd have come yesterday if I'd known what had happened. Poor Aunt Evelyn, but I'm glad it's over, really.'

'She wouldn't have known you, even if you'd come,' I said. 'But now that you're here, I'll go home.'

'Just tell me about these Bodwells first,' Imogen said. 'Are they staying on or what? That woman gives me the creeps. She's so aloof and dignified, she's rather like a stage-housekeeper, don't you think? I don't quite believe in her. And she's already asked me about a reference. I said it would be very convenient for us if she and her husband would stay on for a time, but she didn't seem to want to. I think it's very inconsiderate.'

'I think they're just thinking of their own comfort,' I said. 'They want to feel settled.'

'Don't we all?' Imogen said. 'Well, I suppose I'll be seeing you in the next day or so.'

'Yes, of course.'

I went to the door. I wondered if I ought to go in search of Meg Randall and perhaps take her home with me, leaving Imogen and Patrick to themselves, with only Nigel, who would not be in the least interested in them, prowling quietly about the house, putting imaginary price-tags on objects that he thought might soon belong to him. But deciding to let Meg sink or swim by herself, since sooner or later everyone has to do that, I let myself out of the front door and went to my car.

I was startled to find Meg sitting in it.

She was sitting crouching forward with her head in her hands in the seat beside the driver's, with her fair hair hiding her face. At the sound of the car door being opened her slim body jerked and she sat upright, tossing her hair back.

'Do you mind if I go home with you?' she asked. 'I've got to talk to someone.'

'All right,' I said as I got into the car and started it. 'You're worrying about something more than the betting, aren't you? Is it about the will? Did Mrs Arliss leave her money to you? If so, I don't think you should worry. If she wanted to do that, I don't see what's against it.'

I was driving the car slowly down the drive between the banks of rhododendrons. I did not see Meg's face, but I heard the amazement in her voice.

'To me? Whatever made you think of that?'

'She didn't?'

'Of course not. She liked me, I think, but not as much as all that. Anyway . . .' She stopped.

'What's the trouble then?'

Meg let out a deep sigh.

'They're all thinking so much about the

money, aren't they? It's all they care about. Even Mr Huddleston . . . I saw you at the window, I know you saw them when I did. I'd never have thought it of him, but what can he want with that woman if it isn't her money?'

'A number of people have found her very attractive,' I said.

'She's blowsy and old. Well, I don't mean *old*—I don't suppose she's any older than you are—but you know what I mean.'

'I do indeed. But Patrick isn't so very young himself.' I turned the car into the road that led towards the middle of the town. 'What is it, Meg? What is it you wanted so much to tell me?'

'Only that there isn't any money, you see. There isn't any money at all. A year ago Mrs Arliss put everything she had into annuities. So now she's dead, there isn't anything left. It's all gone. There isn't anything for anyone.'

CHAPTER THREE

I am not good at thinking when I am driving. I know this means that I am not a good driver. I have to concentrate too hard on what I am doing.

Keeping my attention carefully on the road in front of me, which ran between small, semi-detached houses with neat little front gardens, gaudy just now with laburnum and flowering cherry, I drove down towards the old market place of the town.

After a minute or two Meg said querulously, 'Well?'

It sounded as if she felt that her bombshell had turned into a damp squib.

It is surprising how easy it is not to feel worried by the prospect of the financial disappointment of other people.

'I think I'll stop at Whitefield's and buy a few things,' I said. 'You'd better stay and eat with me this evening, then we can talk this over.'

Whitefield's was the supermarket at the corner of the market place, which had a car park in the middle of it, where for once there was some room. Driving in, I popped ten pence in the meter and went into Whitefield's. Meg did not suggest coming in with me, but stayed hunched in her seat, her hair hanging forward again, hiding her face. I was not sure that she had not started crying.

I bought two steaks, a packet of frozen chips and some peas, some *dolce latte,* a loaf of brown bread and a bottle of whisky. I very seldom drink whisky except when I am feeling ill or specially tired, as for instance, after a long journey, but that day I had the feeling of having travelled a long way. If Meg did not feel like whisky, I had sherry in the house. I went back to the car and drove on to Ellsworthy Street. Meg did not speak to me again.

As soon as I opened the door I had the feeling that this had all happened before. There was the smell of cigarette smoke again, too fresh to have been left behind since the morning. So Felix had not kept his promise and gone away.

There were other smells too that told me he was still there, onions, garlic, paprika, wine, all blending into something very rich and savoury, coming from the kitchen. A wonderfully satisfying smell to be greeted by when you were feeling as exhausted as I was, or it should have been, but the truth was that almost immediately I began to wonder if I should be able to eat anything at all.

Felix heard us come in and emerged from the kitchen.

'This is Meg Randall,' I told him. 'She's staying. I hope you've cooked enough for three.' To Meg I added, 'This is that husband

49

of mine who isn't talked about.'

'But—' she began, then stopped and coloured up in the way that she so easily did.

'But you thought we were separated,' I said. 'We are. This is merely a brief interlude. Now let's go into the sitting-room and let him get us something to drink, then we can talk over what you were telling me about in the car.'

She looked deeply embarrassed. She was young enough to feel that the middle-aged ought not to have the complicated sort of relations with one another that sent you floundering out of your depth. Felix saw it at once and was sorry for her.

'Yes, we're separated, but we've always remained the best of friends,' he said, offering her the cliché to make the situation simple for her. 'No need to quarrel just because it happened not to work out too well, living together.'

She looked from one to the other of us and I saw her reflecting that the trouble must have been one of those mysterious sexual maladjustments of the kind about which people almost always refuse to talk honestly, covering up the truth with equivocation and quiet little slanders about one another. In fact, she was wrong. If Felix and I had not agreed pretty well sexually our marriage would not have lasted even as long as it did.

As I went into the sitting-room and she followed me, I said, 'Drinks, now. Whisky,

50

Meg? Sherry? I'm afraid there isn't anything else.'

She chose sherry. I told Felix I wanted whisky, reminding him, in case he should have forgotten how I liked it, that I wanted only a very little water with it. He fetched the drinks, bringing himself a long, very diluted whisky. He had always been a cautious drinker. He could sit among heavy drinking friends and make a single glass last him the whole evening. I think he felt that only a very little too much to drink would make him lose his slender grasp on reality.

'Meg's got some rather strange information about Mrs Arliss,' I told him. 'Go on, Meg, tell us about it.'

She gave Felix a slightly uncertain look as she sat down and took a sip of her sherry.

I said, 'It's all right, he may as well hear it. If we turn him out, he'll only listen at the door.'

'I suppose there isn't any reason why everyone shouldn't hear it now,' she said. 'It's simply that I haven't had time to think things out. Mrs Arliss always made such a point about my never telling anyone about it. She said it was an important part of my job never to talk about her affairs to anyone else. And of course I understood that and I never did. And I didn't mind keeping her gambling to myself, because it seemed to be the only fun she got out of life, and I was sure Miss Dale and Mr Tustin would try to put a stop to it if they knew anything about it. But this other thing was different. I used to feel I owed it to Mr Huddleston to tell him about it. I knew he felt very responsible for her and whenever I saw him he used to ask me about how she was and how I was managing and so on. He really cared about her. And here was this extraordinary thing she'd done and I wasn't allowed to tell him a word about it. It made me feel awful.'

'You mean this putting all her money into annuities,' I said. 'But how could she do that without him knowing about it?'

'He never handled her investments, you see,' she answered. 'There's a firm of accountants who've managed her income tax for her for years and years and they've an investment department and she got them to make all the arrangements for her. She told me they advised her against it, but she'd made up her own mind that annuities were the way to get the largest possible income from her capital and pay the least income tax and she insisted on going ahead with her scheme. She more or less told me once she didn't mind if she left nothing behind for anyone to inherit, only I think she was sorry about that at the end, because only a few days ago she told me she meant to do the right thing by Miss Dale, her own sister's child, but I don't know what she meant by that.'

'Just a minute,' Felix said, nursing his pale drink. 'I missed the first part of this conversation. Do you mean Mrs Arliss's money is all in annuities which of course stop with her death and so there's nothing left for the relatives?'

Meg nodded. 'And I'm sure—I'm sure now—that I ought to have told Mr Huddleston about it, so that he could have stopped her. I don't know quite how I'm going to face him now. He thought she trusted him, you know, because obviously she enjoyed his company. She loved it when he came to see her. But she did say to me he wasn't the man his father was and she didn't think he was reliable. I—I always thought she was wrong and I told her so, but she said I was—well, that doesn't matter. I dare say I was wrong. Perhaps he isn't reliable. All the same, I've got a feeling I ought to have let him know what she was doing.'

'What I don't understand,' I said, 'is why she did it. Even if she'd put her money into a mere deposit account, it would have brought her far more than she needed to live on.'

'Ah,' Felix said, giving one of his knowing smiles, 'it was hatred, of course. Sheer hatred of her dear niece and nephew, to whom she'd never meant anything but money. She must have felt wonderful, lying there dying, knowing how she'd cheated them. I can't help admiring her. It was a neat trick she played them.'

'I don't think it was like that at all,' Meg said. 'I think really at the back of her mind she was scared of her passion for gambling and thought she might suddenly be left with no money at all. Doesn't that sometimes happen to old people? They get absolutely convinced they're poor when really they're still very rich. So she wanted to put her money where even she herself couldn't touch it, but where she could be sure it would go on bringing her in a nice, steady income.'

'No, my dear,' Felix said. 'That's a kind way to think of it and I'm sure it comes naturally to you to think kindly of others, unlike my dear wife who always sees the worst in everyone, or at any rate in me. But the truth is, Mrs Arliss played her relatives a beautiful con trick, keeping their attention on her all this time when she knew perfectly well there wasn't going to be anything in it for them. Perhaps hatred's a rather strong word for it, but at least you could call it spite. You see, she never pretended to Virginia, whom she was really fond of, that she was ever going to leave her anything. She was quite open and above-board with her. But this gambling business is news to me. I missed that part of the conversation too.'

'She liked betting on horses, that's all,' I said. 'And she was afraid that if Imogen and Nigel found out, they'd get a power of attorney and stop her touching her own money.'

'I see. Yes, certainly have her certified. Plainly it's most wrong to gamble when one's over eighty. That would have been the obvious course for them to take. That's what I'd have done in their place. But they never found out about it, is that it?'

'No, I never said a word about it to anyone until today,' Meg said. 'But I hated it, I simply hated it! I hate secrets. I like to be open with everyone. I don't like having to remember the things I mustn't say. It felt specially awful not saying anything about it to Patrick when he was—well, at least he seemed to be—fond of Mrs Arliss for herself. But I could be wrong about that, I suppose. I'm afraid I'm not very good at understanding people.'

She was not aware how the word Patrick had slipped out, instead of the formal Mr Huddleston that she had been careful to use until then, but of course Felix did not miss it. He gave me a swift, questioning look, raising his thick, golden eyebrows. Then he turned back to Meg.

'Well, there's the house,' he said consolingly, 'and that might be worth a hundred thousand in times like these. So someone will do all right.'

'No,' she said.

'No?'

'No. You can get a sort of annuity on a house and get paid interest on it while you live, but when you die it goes to the insurance company.'

'And she did that too?'

She nodded. 'There's absolutely nothing left.'

He gave a little chuckle. 'She was thorough, wasn't she? You have to admire her.'

'Of course there's still the furniture,' I said. 'She can't have disposed of that. Not that much of it's really good, but I expect it'll fetch some thousands. Then there's the Rolls. That must be worth a fair amount too.'

'And the miniatures,' Felix said. 'They're certainly the most valuable thing in the house. I wonder who inherits them.'

I had forgotten about Mr Arliss's collection of miniatures. I knew nothing about their value or their aesthetic merits. I had realized, from the clothes of the people who had sat for them, that they belonged to the late eighteenth and early nineteenth centuries, and I had always thought them charming, without ever having paid much attention to them. Mrs Arliss had sometimes spoken of them, but more because of what the collecting of them had meant to her husband than because they had meant much to her in themselves. Hanging on a wall of the drawing-room, as they did, they were surprisingly exposed to any casual thief, supposing they were valuable.

'You said just now she told you she meant to do the right thing by Imogen, didn't you?' I said. 'But Patrick told me he thought she'd left everything to Imogen as it was. There were some legacies for one or two other people, he said, but everything else went to Imogen. If there actually wasn't anything, it looks almost as if Mrs Arliss was more confused at the end than we thought.'

'I don't think so,' Meg said. 'But I know she telephoned him last Monday and he came to see her on Tuesday and I wondered at the time if she was altering her will again. I was out myself, having my hair done, so I didn't see him, but he came again next day, just to ask how she was, and he told me then she'd got him to destroy the last will she'd made. I suppose in that one she'd left her money to Mr Tustin, and I thought it was odd, since I knew she hadn't any money. Yet her mind seemed perfectly normal to me.'

'Perhaps she sometimes forgot about things like those annuities,' Felix said, 'and realized she did and felt more frightened by it than she wanted anyone to know, because she had the thought of that power of attorney hanging over her. After all, her income must have been quite substantial, and if Imogen and Nigel could have got their hands on the spending of it, they might have benefited very pleasantly.'

'But what am I to do now?' Meg pleaded with us to tell her. 'Mr Huddleston's got to know about it, hasn't he, because he's an executor? So please, Mrs Freer, couldn't you tell him for me?'

'What would be the good of that?' I asked. 'He'd still have to come to you to hear the whole story.'

'Yes, but . . .' She twisted her fingers

together. They were long and slender and very expressive of her desperation. 'If you could tell him why I didn't tell him anything about it before . . . If you told him how bad I feel about it . . . No, don't do that. I don't want to excuse myself to him about anything. The truth is, I don't want to talk to him any more than I can help at the moment. It's stupid of me, but he's—well, a different person from what I thought him.'

She was still obsessed with the picture in her mind of Patrick and Imogen locked in each other's arms. Felix, of course, guessed what was the matter with her and putting a hand on her shoulder, patted it reassuringly. The physical contact seemed to do her good and she gave him a smile, rather a wan one, but at least it took some of the misery out of her face.

'You mustn't worry,' he said. 'In my opinion, your behaviour's been exemplary. Huddleston can't possibly criticize you. You were trusted by your employer and you were faithful to that trust. I wish I had a secretary in whom I knew for certain I could repose such confidence.'

'Have you a secretary at all,' I asked, 'trustworthy or comfortably crooked?'

'I have an excellent girl called Clementine,' he replied stiffly. 'If I hadn't, or if I had any real fault to find with her, I should be offering this charming girl her post and hoping devoutly I could persuade her to fill it. I immensely admire her loyalty and conscientiousness. But Clementine is adequate and does her best, so dismissing her would be unjust. No, I can only advise you, my dear, to tell Huddleston everything and trust to his good sense not to blame you in any way.'

To me, of course, this was merely Felix in his role of responsible business man, of man of affairs, experienced in the ways of the world and warm-heartedly glad to give the benefit of that experience to a young and bewildered girl. It was all too familiar to me and I thought that even someone as young and bewildered as Meg must see through it. But what I was forgetting was that once I had failed to see through it myself. Had I been so very much simpler myself then, I wondered, or had his technique become cruder? In any case, it did not matter. The reassurance he had given Meg was kindly meant and at least he had not gone quite so far as to offer her the job of the almost certainly non-existent Clementine.

'Now you must have another drink,' he said, 'while I dish up. I'm a little anxious about my stew because I couldn't find the peppercorns. I don't really know my way about Virginia's kitchen and for all I know there simply aren't any peppercorns in it and unluckily it didn't occur to me to buy any when I was out shopping this morning. But I hope you'll forgive any deficiencies on the grounds that I'm unfamiliar with my surroundings.'

He got up and refilled our glasses, then

disappeared into the kitchen.

We ate there presently, the concoction that Felix had modestly called a stew turning out to be as delicious as the odours with which it had filled the house. At first I thought that I had no appetite and would not possibly be able to eat anything as rich and highly flavoured, but there I was wrong. It was just what I needed. The burgundy that he had bought also helped to bring on a feeling of drowsy calm. We ended the meal with a variety of interesting cheeses which he had discovered, I could not imagine where, in Allingford.

He did most of the talking, telling Meg how he had once worked for an oil company in Iran and of the hardships and remarkable rewards of life there. I had never heard this particular story before and listened with a dreamy kind of interest. I supposed that he had recently had an encounter, perhaps in some London pub, with an oil man from Iran and was giving us a boiled-down version of the man's account of his own life. Afterwards Felix offered to drive Meg back to the Arliss house. She looked as if she would have liked to stay on with us for the rest of the evening, but Felix dropped a remark about how tired I was looking and how I ought to go to bed at once and she took the hint, thanked us for letting her talk so much and left. They had to go in my car, as Felix had arrived by bus, after supposedly delivering his second-hand car to a customer in the neighbourhood. I wished I knew if that had really happened, or if it had been one of his fictions, intended to cover up I did not know what.

While they were gone I stacked the dishwasher, went upstairs, got into my nightdress and dressing-gown and was lying on the sofa in the sitting-room, looking idly through a newspaper, when Felix returned.

He sat down, lit a cigarette and said, 'That girl's in love with Huddleston, isn't she?'

'That's my impression,' I said.

'How does he respond?'

'I don't think he knows she exists.'

'Pity. She's charming.'

I could have told him about the scene between Patrick and Imogen that both Meg and I had witnessed, but I had long ago got out of the habit of telling Felix any more than I could help. He was capable of twisting the most casual statements into meanings that no one had intended. However, I was feeling mellower towards him than I usually did. His kindliness to Meg and his stew and his wine had made me admit to myself that he had certain virtues. I found that I even liked the feeling of seeing another human being, and a man at that, sitting in the chair facing me, instead of having the quiet room all to myself.

He tapped ash into the saucer on the floor at his feet. 'You really do look dreadfully tired,' he said. 'Why don't you go to bed.'

'I'll go in a minute,' I said. 'I just wanted to be sure you'd lock up properly.'

It felt very domesticated.

'It's all right, I've shot the bolts.' He gave me a frowning look. 'I'm sure you had that dressing-gown when I saw you last.'

'Probably I had,' I said. 'I've had it a good long time.'

'Why don't you get something more interesting?'

'Why should I, when there's no one but me to see it? This one is very comfortable.'

'Do you know why you put it on this evening and came down and lay around in it? It was just to show that I'm not of any importance to you. But even if I'm not, I don't like seeing you let yourself go to pieces. You're still an attractive woman. You shouldn't let go so easily.'

'Let go of what?'

'Well, perhaps the hopes of a happy marriage. Happier than the last one. You know, I often worry about you. I don't like the feeling that perhaps I've ruined your life. I'd like to see you make a fresh start some time.'

'You don't have to worry,' I said. 'I'm managing quite nicely. It's your own life you've ruined. And sometimes I worry about that myself. Take that story about having been an oil man in Iran, for instance. You must really have listened attentively to whomever it was that gave you all the detail that made it sound so convincing, and if ever you'd put a fraction of that concentration into some proper job, you'd have ended up a vice-president of something, or a famous barrister, or a noted surgeon, or almost anything you aimed at. You've plenty of talent, only you've never used it in any rational way.'

'I only told the girl that story because I thought she needed distracting,' he said, missing my point, probably deliberately. We had been over this ground too often for him not to know what I meant. 'I was sorry for her. As I said, a charming girl. Loyalty's a very attractive quality. Of course, I didn't know for sure how much I told her about the oil business was accurate. I didn't altogether trust the man who told me about it. You'd be surprised how many people there are around who tell you the most appalling lies. Honestly, I'm not the only one. And all mine are harmless, now aren't they? But as I was telling you, I worry about you a good deal. Living alone like this can't be good for you, and I know it's my fault. My shortcomings have scarred you for life. I'm very sorry about it. It's a heavy load on my conscience.'

He was probably speaking the truth. He had a quite active conscience, though it worked in a mysterious way.

'I shouldn't worry,' I said. 'I'm surprisingly contented. And in a way, I'd say we've a rather pleasant relationship. I don't know anyone I can be as comfortably unkind to as I can to you and that's a great safety-valve. Only I wish I knew why you really came here to see me.'

His slanting eyelids flickered, as if, for a moment, he was on the edge of telling me something. But if so, he changed his mind.

'Just that I was in the neighbourhood and thought what a waste it'd be not to come in and see you,' he said. 'I suppose you'd like me to leave tomorrow.'

'Unless you've anything special to stay for.' I got to my feet. 'You've made up a bed in the spare room, have you?'

'Yes, and I'll see you in the morning.'

'Good night, then.'

'Good night.'

I went upstairs, got into bed and must have been asleep by the time my head touched the pillow.

In the morning Felix brought me a cup of tea in bed. He had always been good at doing that and I enjoyed the luxury of it. Then he cooked the breakfast. I had to hurry over it, because it was my day at the clinic and I had not got started as early as I should.

When I left the house he followed me out to the car, kissed me on one ear and said, 'Well, goodbye, and thanks for the hospitality. Perhaps I'll come again some time, just to see how you're making out. I've a feeling you're lonelier than you admit.'

It gave me a pang, because of course I had

not been hospitable. But I was not prepared to admit that I felt unduly lonely. Too many people I know can persuade themselves that they suffer miseries of loneliness while also complaining of feeling so hemmed in and badgered by other people that they develop a frantic, self-pitying revulsion from human company. I knew that I had a tendency to do this myself, but generally tried to control it. I waved a hand to Felix as I drove off to show him that my feelings towards him just then were friendly and arrived only about ten minutes late at the clinic.

I need not have said goodbye. When I arrived home about half past five that evening, after a fuller, rather more demanding day than usual, Felix was still there. As soon as I opened the door I smelt the familiar cigarette smoke and found him, as I had the day before, stretched out on the sofa. Except for keeping a cigarette dangling between his fingers, he was doing nothing. He had a great capacity for idleness. Sometimes he spent hours at a time in what I took to be absorbing daydreams. If I had found that he had been reading a book, or even a newspaper, it would have surprised me.

'I had second thoughts after you'd gone,' he said apologetically. 'I thought perhaps I'd stay for the funeral. I was fond of the old girl, you know, and I think she had a soft spot for me.'

'Now that's something I really don't want,' I said, exasperated. 'The complications of our marriage have always been hard enough to explain to the family and I don't want them getting it into their heads that we're patching things up.'

'Would it matter if they did think that?' he asked.

'Yes, it bores and annoys me when people start probing into our private mysteries, as they certainly would. So I'd sooner not give them the opportunity to start raising their eyebrows, particularly at a funeral.'

He sighed. 'All right, no funeral. But I can stay here the night again, can't I? I thought we might go out to dinner.'

'There are two steaks in the fridge,' I said. 'I bought them yesterday for Meg and me before I knew you'd taken over the cooking. We can have those. I don't feel like going out.'

'All right, I'll attend to them. And you'd like a drink now, I expect. Whisky again?'

'Sherry tonight, thank you.'

'Good, I'm glad of that. Yesterday I thought you might be making a habit of drinking whisky and that's dangerous, you know, if you live on your own. You can slip into the way of quietly tippling away all day and before you know where you are you're an alcoholic. I could tell you of several cases of it. Very sad cases.'

'I am not an alcoholic and I find your solicitude for me perfectly revolting,' I said.

'I'm so sorry, I meant well,' he said. 'Now sit

66

down and relax and I'll get that sherry.'

He went out.

Sitting down, I kicked off my shoes, leant back and closed my eyes, yawned once or twice, reflected that there was some virtue in being waited on and would have been asleep in another moment if I had not been jerked wide awake by the ringing of the front doorbell.

I pushed my feet back into my shoes, got up and went to the door. Imogen stood there. Her car was parked at the gate. Even before I had let her into the house I realized that there was something unusual about her. She was wearing the same grey suit that she had worn the day before, her make-up was as careful as ever, her hair was sleek and trim. Yet she looked distraught. Her gaze at me was so fixed that her eyes seemed actually to be protruding. That something was wrong with her was obvious and not too surprisingly I could guess what it was.

'I'm sorry to burst in on you like this,' she said as I took her into the sitting-room, 'but I must talk to you. That treacherous little bitch, Meg Randall, has been talking to you, hasn't she? I want to know what she said.'

'Sit down,' I said, 'and let's have a drink. Incidentally, I don't think Meg's treacherous or a bitch, but a rather nice girl.'

Imogen did not sit down but started to roam restlessly about the room.

'A treacherous little bitch,' she repeated

through her teeth. 'All right, whisky. The point is, there ought to be some way of dealing with her. Patrick says there isn't, that we'll just have to accept things the way they are, but I can't believe it. There must be something we can do.'

Her voice was hoarse with excitement. I left her and went into the dining-room, where I kept the drinks. Felix was there with my sherry poured out and he was already pouring out a whisky for Imogen, having evidently heard all that she had said since she had come into the house.

He whispered to me, 'It's all right, I won't crash in on you. You'd sooner I didn't, wouldn't you?'

'On the whole, yes,' I said. 'She's in quite enough of a state as it is.'

'Can you blame her? It's a very unnerving thing, losing money you've counted on.'

He handed me the glasses for Imogen and myself and I carried them into the sitting-room. I knew that he would probably listen at the door, so closing it behind me after I had put down the two glasses was only a formality, but at least Imogen need not know that he was there. He and she had never been even moderately friendly. They seemed to see through each other with devastating clarity and had a trick of needling one another quite offensively, which today, I could easily imagine, might make Imogen completely lose her temper, a thing that I had witnessed a few times and had not enjoyed.

When I gave her her drink she sat down and fixed her intense gaze on my face.

'You know there's no money, don't you?' she said.

'Yes,' I said, 'Meg told me yesterday evening.'

'That's the first you knew of it?'

'Yes.'

'Because if I thought you'd known about it too . . .' Her glare threatened me with dreadful things.

'Calm down,' I said. 'Even if I had, there wouldn't be anything you could do about it, would there? But I didn't. It came as just as much of a surprise to me as it did to you.'

'It couldn't have. You weren't expecting anything for yourself, were you?'

'Well, no, I'm not directly affected. But I was truly astonished. But I don't blame Meg in the least for telling nobody. She was merely doing her duty, as she saw it, by Mrs Arliss.'

'She ought to have told Patrick about it, then perhaps he could have prevented it. The wretched girl must have seen that Aunt Evelyn wasn't in her right mind any more and that she ought to be looked after. The child had no right to take so much responsibility on herself. She's too young and inexperienced. Of course, I never trusted her myself. I wouldn't be at all surprised if she's been getting away all these months with rather more than her pay. But Patrick assured me she was all right. She'd fallen for him for one thing, and he never dreamt she'd keep anything important from him. That's his vanity. I laughed at him about it when he told me and he got into a pretty black rage. Not that he showed it, he's too smooth, but Meg knew what he'd feel about the whole thing when he found out and I could see that she was dead scared of telling him anything. Serves her right. I imagine by now she's lost any illusions she had about his feelings for her.'

It almost sounded as if Imogen was jealous of Meg.

'Weren't you there when she told him?' I asked.

'No, she did it on the telephone this morning while I was still in bed, but I saw the state she was in later and he told me he'd immediately made some enquiries at those accountants of Aunt Evelyn's and found Meg had told him the truth. There's nothing left. And the sickening thing is, in her will Aunt Evelyn left everything to me—everything that counts. And there isn't anything.'

'Well, I'm awfully sorry about it,' I said. 'It must be a very nasty blow. But after all, there's the Rolls and there's the furniture and there are those miniatures, which may be quite valuable. There'll be at least several thousands for you when you sell up.'

'Several thousands!' she said contemptuously. 'How far d'you think they'll go nowadays? It's practically nothing.'

'I'd be very happy myself if someone left me a nothing like that,' I said. 'And after all, Imogen, you aren't a poor woman. I know it's a shock, but allowing for taxation and all, it isn't going to make such a tremendous difference to you really. It'll be best just to accept the situation without letting yourself get too upset.'

She gave me a strange, blank look which I found oddly frightening, there was such an intensity of feeling behind it. I did not know what the feeling was, rage, or a wild kind of anxiety, or just possibly despair, though the thought that that was what it might be was very puzzling.

'You don't understand,' she said in a dull voice.

'I'm sorry,' I said. 'I wish I could say something to help. You aren't in any real trouble, are you, Imogen?'

I knew that her mother and Mrs Arliss had inherited the same amount from their parents and that Mrs Arliss had then married a rich man and Mrs Dale a poor one, so that Imogen had not inherited as much from her mother as she had been hoping for from Mrs Arliss, but all the same, she had always seemed to me to have more than enough for her needs. She had never been driven to looking for a job, for instance.

'Nothing you could call trouble,' she answered in the same flat tone. 'No, I know I'm being stupid. You can't help, even if you'd like to. I thought perhaps you could. I thought if you said Aunt Evelyn had been unbalanced for some time those annuities might be cancelled or something . . . But you're right and so is Patrick, there's nothing to do but accept the situation. So for one thing I'll have to sell my house and go to some horrible little flat in the suburbs—I think that's the thing I dread most—because an old house like mine takes a lot of keeping up, you know. I got some dry rot in the basement last year and it cost the earth to put right. And the rates go up and up and somehow I always have an overdraft, I don't know why. I suppose it's inflation. And—oh, there are other things. But nothing you could call trouble—oh no.'

There was a mocking note in her voice as she said it, as if she was telling me that I really did not know what trouble was. After that she finished her drink quickly and left.

Felix left the next morning. The funeral was at eleven o'clock, so I was able to drive him to the station, leaving him at the booking-office, before driving on to St Hilary's. There was a long line of cars outside the church, for Mrs Arliss, if she had been a woman with few intimate friends, had had many contacts with people who in one way or another were under obligations to her. The church was full. I was shown to a seat next to Meg Randall, who had Paul Goss, Imogen's nephew, on the other side of her. I did not know him well. As a child he had often been sent for his holidays to stay with Mrs Arliss, but as he grew up and presumably had had more to say himself about how his holidays should be spent, he had come to visit her less and less often. This had hurt her, but I suppose that for someone of his age it must have been pretty boring to spend two or three weeks with an old woman of over eighty.

He was twenty-four now, tall, broad-shouldered and good-looking in much the same way as Imogen. That is to say, he had her thick, dark hair, a high colour and bright, dark eyes. He had recently taken a degree in history at Bristol University and for the last few months had been working for a publisher of historical and sociological textbooks. Both his parents were dead. His mother, Imogen's sister, had been killed in a car-crash when he was about fifteen and his father had died of a coronary three years later. Imogen had given him a home for some time, but he now lived by himself in a flat in Battersea.

Imogen was in the pew in front of us, with Patrick Huddleston beside her, but there was no sign of Nigel. He arrived late, panting slightly, but as always walking sedately, looking assured that the service could not start without him. The Bodwells were not there. The Reverend Matthew Bailey conducted the service in his hushed, whispering voice, directing it, it seemed, at a spot on the floor before him. Afterwards most of the crowd that had been in the church melted away and only a few went on to the cemetery.

There was a cold east wind blowing that bore away most of the vicar's words into the empty air. The sunshine of the last few days had gone and low, grey, hurrying clouds covered the sky. The trees at the edge of the cemetery tossed their branches, making rasping sounds as they brushed against one another. The coffin, as it was lowered into the hole in the ground, the rawness of which had been hidden from the view by a coverlet of artificial emerald green grass, looked strangely small. Mrs Arliss had not been a particularly small woman, yet death seemed to have shrunk her.

When the time came for earth to be scattered on the coffin, Mr Robertson, or perhaps it was Mr Jarvis, the Funeral Director, took a small plastic bag out of his pocket, which contained what looked like dehydrated sand, inserted his fingers into the bag and delicately sprinkled a few grains of this substance on the coffin lid. I was so intrigued by this odd, sterilized version of the old ceremony that I paid almost no attention to the majesty of the words that went with it. But even if I had tried to listen, they would have been carried away from me in the teeth of the east wind. Even in the time that we waited by the graveside the day grew wilder. I thought that there might well be a storm before evening.

As we all went towards our cars, Imogen gripped my arm.

'You'll come back with us, won't you?' she said.

'If that's what you want,' I answered.

'There'll be lunch of a sort. The Bodwells said they'd get it. Then I think I'll go home. There's not much point in staying, is there? Patrick can settle everything and you can help him if he needs it. I don't know what Nigel and Paul are intending to do, but I want to get away. I've never liked staying here, you know. Visiting Aunt Evelyn always got on my nerves. She knew it, of course, and that's why she treated me as she did. If I'd put on a better show she mightn't have done it, but I've never been any good at hiding my feelings.' She gave a sharp sigh. 'Thank God the funeral's over, anyway. And I'll just have to get used to the idea that that's that. Perhaps things won't really turn out as badly as I think.'

She let go of my arm and went to one of the stately black limousines laid on by Messrs. Robertson and Jarvis.

I followed in my car. By the time that we reached the house it had begun to rain and there was an almost wintry feeling in the air, or so it seemed to me as I went into the house. It had always been a cold house, even when there were cheerful fires burning, and today it looked abnormally desolate. I realized that the desolation was mostly in my own mind and that at last I was beginning to feel the pain of losing my old friend, but still there was a chill in the big, silent rooms that made me shiver.

Also, there was no lunch. The long table in the dining-room was bare. There were no Bodwells either and the miniatures from the drawing-room wall were gone too. There were only rows of small, pale oblongs on the wallpaper to show where they had hung for so many years.

CHAPTER FOUR

Strangely enough, it seemed far worse at first that there was no lunch waiting for us than that the miniatures had gone. It might have been thought, from the way that we craved for food, that we had been starved for a week. Nigel busied himself with drinks, but these hardly took the edge off our hunger. At odd times I saw someone take a worried glance at the wall where the miniatures had hung and Patrick muttered something about the police, yet no one seemed to want to take active steps about the matter until the problem had been solved of whether we were going to be fed.

Presently this was solved by Meg, assisted by Paul, who between them produced some cold roast beef, a limp-looking salad and some bread and cheese. For such a windy, cheerless day it was a depressingly chilly meal. Nigel disappeared into the cellars and after a little while reappeared with two bottles of *Château Neuf du Pape,* which he said would of course not be at the right temperature, but would be better than nothing. I was not sure that he was right. The wine seemed, if anything, to add to the chill in the atmosphere. When we had finished, Meg made coffee, which at least was hot, and leaving the debris of the meal spread over the table, as if we had forgotten that there was now no Mrs Bodwell to clear up after us, we filed back into the drawing-room.

There was no longer any avoiding the matter of the miniatures. Patrick went to the telephone. Imogen asked him whom he was going to call and he said of course the police.

She said that the idea of talking to the police just then was really too much to be faced.

'I want to go and lie down,' she said. 'And who wants the damned things back anyway?'

'Nigel may,' Patrick said. 'Mrs Arliss left them to him. At least he may want the insurance on them, and we've got to call the police if he does.'

'As a matter of fact . . .' Meg said, stopped abruptly in that way that she had and looked as if she wished she had not spoken.

'Yes?' Patrick asked in a rather impatient tone, his hand still on the telephone.

'I don't think they're insured at all,' she said. 'Mrs Arliss stopped bothering about paying the premiums. She said it wasn't worth while. I tried to get her to sign the cheques, but she said what did it matter and she kept putting it off, saying she'd do it another day, but she never did.'

'Well, Nigel,' Patrick said, 'shall I telephone the police to see if they can pick up the Bodwells before they vanish, or shall we do nothing about it?'

'She'd left them to me?' Nigel said, looking

78

surprised and somehow alarmed, as if he found something abnormal in this. 'Dear me, I thought she'd left everything to Imogen. Didn't you say so the other day?'

'I hadn't checked up,' Patrick said. 'I knew Imogen was the residuary legatee, but I didn't remember the details of the legacies. But I've gone into it since and I found Mrs Arliss left her husband's collection of miniatures to you and his books to Paul and what was left to Imogen. But as you all know, there's nothing left. And if Meg's right now about the insurance having lapsed, I'm afraid there'll be nothing for you unless we can get the miniatures back.'

'So Paul's the only one who benefits at all and that not very much. Those books are nothing special. The old devil!' Imogen exploded. 'She had it in for all of us, didn't she? She didn't want any of us to gain by her death.'

'She couldn't have known the miniatures were going to be stolen, could she?' Patrick said. 'You aren't suggesting she arranged that with the Bodwells in advance of her death.'

'I suppose not, but why in hell couldn't this stupid girl here have told us how senile the old woman had become?' Imogen demanded. 'She'd got quite irresponsible. You'd no right to keep all these things to yourself, Meg.'

'Oh, I don't think we can blame Meg for not having warned us,' Nigel said. 'She's very

79

young to have to carry such a responsibility. If she felt that above all things she must be loyal to Mrs Arliss, I think it's to her credit.'

Patrick had let go of the telephone.

'I think I'm more than a bit to blame myself for the way things have turned out,' he said. 'Mrs Arliss sent for me last Monday and made me destroy a will she'd made about a year ago in which she left the miniatures to Imogen and the residue to Nigel. She told me she wanted to do right by Imogen, who was her own flesh and blood, and so she wanted her earlier will to stand. I imagined, of course, she wanted to leave the bulk of her estate to Imogen and only legacies to Nigel and Paul and I'm sure, in fact, that's what she believed she was doing. She'd forgotten she hadn't any estate to leave. I agree with Imogen that she was far more senile than any of us realized. However, I agree with Nigel that we shouldn't blame Meg for not having warned us. She couldn't possibly have understood the complexity of the situation. Now, shall I call the police, Nigel?'

'Yes, yes,' Nigel said. 'I share Imogen's dislike of the idea of having them here today, but of course it's unavoidable. I'll be grateful if you'll call them, Patrick.'

'I know Detective-Inspector Roper,' Patrick said. 'He's a very sound man. I'll ask for him.'

He picked up the telephone, dialled, asked for the Detective-Inspector and when he had been connected, spoke briefly, had a brief answer, said a word of thanks and put the telephone down again.

'There'll be someone here in a few minutes,' he said. 'Meanwhile, do any of you know anything about these miniatures? I mean about the artists who painted them, their dates and so on. The police are going to want as full a description of them as possible. I've seen them myself I don't know how often, but I doubt if I could identify a single one of them.'

'Nor could I,' Imogen said. 'They were just a lot of simpering females to me. What I personally would like to know is a little about the Bodwells. How did they get this job with Aunt Evelyn in the first place? Did they just come out of the blue, or had they any references? None of us knows anything much about them, do we?'

'They came with an excellent reference,' Patrick said. 'I checked it myself. They'd worked for about seven years for an elderly couple and only left them because these people were going to live in Portugal. They'd given the Bodwells a written reference, but I telephoned and spoke to the man about them—Sir Oswald Smith-Something—I can't remember his name exactly, but I'll have a record of it somewhere—and he couldn't praise the Bodwells enough.'

'Smith-Ogilvie?' I asked before I could stop myself.

Patrick turned to me with a look of surprise.

81

'Yes, that's right. How clever of you to remember. I suppose I told you about it.'

'Yes,' I said, 'I suppose you must have.'

But he had never said a word about it and I felt my face redden with confusion and felt furious with myself for what I had blurted out. It had slipped out before I had had time to think. For the name Oswald Smith-Ogilvie was dreadfully familiar to me. It was an alias of which Felix was particularly fond. On one occasion, before he had discovered that he could not count on me to play his kind of game for him, I had found myself registered at a hotel as Lady Smith-Ogilvie. I had left the same evening, instead of staying the fortnight that we had intended, and he had followed me home next day, querulously puzzled at why I should have objected to my social promotion. He had meant nothing dishonest by it, he had said. The dishonesty, if any, so he had insisted, was on the part of the kind of people who ran hotels, who would give you far better service if you gave yourself a title and a hyphenated name than if you were plain Mr and Mrs Freer. It was all part of the deplorable British class system, he had said, which in reality was just a gigantic con trick and which you were a fool to be taken in by. He had me almost convinced by the time he had finished, but luckily he had never tried to involve me again in the doings of Sir Oswald.

Not until now, that was to say. Not until it

had emerged that the Bodwells were friends of his, as well as being thieves. I was involved in that and needed to think quickly about how much I meant to say about it.

Of course, I could have told the police everything. I could have given them Felix's address and told them that they would almost certainly be able to find out from him where to look for the Bodwells. But there is something about having been married to a man which makes it extraordinarily difficult to let anyone else know the full extent of his misdoings. I had always had a feeling that I must cover up for Felix when I could. Yet at the same time I usually tried not to let him get away with too much. I had at least always been careful, after our early days when I had still believed that I might be able to cure him just by loving him, not to let him think that he had deluded me in any respect. But that was about as far as I had ever gone and though naturally it had had very little effect on him, I had never felt tempted to take anyone else into my confidence about his lies and minor crimes and general crookedness.

In the end I said nothing to the police about him or Sir Oswald Smith-Ogilvie. There was no difficulty about this, because they were not expecting anything from me. They arrived only about a quarter of an hour after Patrick had telephoned, first a young detective-sergeant and a uniformed constable, then Patrick's friend, Detective-Inspector Roper, a heavily built man with a smooth, round face, dark hair receding from a bulging forehead, the sort of staring eyes that people often associate, quite mistakenly, with murderous tendencies, a thick neck and a cold, incisive voice. He asked us for our descriptions of the Bodwells, paying most attention to Meg's, partly because she had seen more of them than any of the rest of us, but also because it was plain that she had the power of detailed observation often possessed by the young. She had noticed far more about both Bodwells than I was able to recall. But when it came to describing the missing miniatures she had nothing to say. The only one who had some knowledge of them was Nigel.

'I think there were about thirty of them,' he said, 'but I can't make any guess at what their value is likely to be in these inflationary times. Perhaps somewhere between thirty and forty thousand, though of course they didn't cost nearly that when my uncle bought them. There were several Larboroughs—he was one of the most noted miniaturists of the end of the eighteenth century—and some by the Frenchman, De Ligne, a little later in date, but very fine work, and some particularly charming portraits by Roselli, an Italian, also of about the same period. They were all painted on ivory and I think without exception were of women—young women mostly—and for some reason that increases their value. Miniatures of men, with the exception of some of those of great figures—you'll know the famous one of Cromwell, for instance, a wonderful thing—have never been as popular as those of women. Collectors seem to be particularly partial to pretty ladies.'

I saw the sergeant smile fleetingly, I supposed at Nigel's assumption that Inspector Roper would be acquainted with a miniature of Cromwell, or of anybody else, however eminent. But in an instant the sergeant's face was solemn again. He was a nice-looking young man with curly fair hair, a square, well-tanned face and blue eyes that looked too innocent for someone who had to dabble daily in the murky waters of crime. The constable with him was older than he was, a responsible-looking man, who, if he had not been in uniform, might have easily been mistaken for a bank manager. Except that he occasionally whispered to the sergeant, I did not hear him make a single remark from the time that he entered the house until he left it. The sergeant also did not say much, but was put in charge by Mr Roper of having the kitchen and the Bodwells' bedroom fingerprinted, and of taking all our fingerprints too, so that none of them should be confused with any left by the Bodwells.

Time passed slowly. After a while Meg came and sat beside me and almost in a whisper, as if she felt that what she had to say was something that the police should not overhear, remarked to me, 'I like him tremendously.'

'Who?' I asked. 'Inspector Roper?'

'No, no, Felix. He's got terrific charm.'

'I've always thought so myself,' I said.

'He's had an adventurous life, hasn't he?' she went on. 'He told me quite a lot about it.'

'I'm sure he didn't tell you half.'

'It somehow seems a pity . . .' She checked herself. It was another of her half sentences that she was afraid to finish.

I finished it for her. 'That we broke up? Well, these things happen. Our approach to life was too different.'

'Was he away too much?' she asked. 'I think if I'd been you I'd have gone with him. But if you don't care for travel, I suppose it might be difficult.'

'Just which of his trips were you thinking of?' I asked.

'That trip on skis across the Greenland ice-cap, for one,' she said.

'I can't ski.'

'He made it sound fabulous.'

'I'm sure he did.'

'Such wonderful sunsets, he said. But you resented it, I suppose—I mean, that he'd go away like that all by himself and leave you behind.'

'No, I never really resented that. It always suited me best to be left behind.'

'Then why . . .? Oh, I know I oughtn't to be talking like this. It's none of my business.'

'It doesn't matter. I'm glad you liked him.'

She gave me a puzzled look. It was clear that she found my attitude bewildering, but she dropped the subject. It was about five o'clock when at last I was able to leave the house and go home.

For once I should have been quite glad to find Felix there, but the house was empty. It was not that I should have liked to find out what he knew about the Bodwells, but after the stress of the day, it would have been pleasant to be brought a drink by him and just let him talk any nonsense that came into his head. But except for the whistling of the wind in the chimney, the house was silent.

I decided it was another day for whisky, made myself a drink, carried it into the sitting-room, where I switched on the electric fire, because, for May, it felt astonishingly cold, and settled down beside it, wondering what I should cook for my supper. A boiled egg seemed as good an idea as any. And I need not hurry about getting it. I could sit here, drink and unwind, for as long as I chose, doing my best to let my mind become a soothing blank. After all, I soon began to feel, I was glad that Felix was not with me. If he had been, I knew that I should have started arguing with him, trying to get the truth about the Bodwells out of him and refusing to believe anything that he told me. Being alone was far more restful than that hopelessly distracting kind of argument. But I had not been alone for more than half an hour when the front doorbell rang.

I was glad to see that it was Paul. If I did not know him well, at least there was nothing complicated in our relationship. Nothing to dodge, nothing to be cautious and evasive about.

I said, 'How did you get here? You haven't a car, have you?'

'I walked,' he said. 'I like to walk.'

I took him into the sitting-room, gave him a drink and waited for him to tell me why he had come. I guessed that it was probably for advice of some sort, perhaps something to do with the books that Mrs Arliss had left him, how to sell them in Allingford, perhaps, or some other minor practical matter.

It startled me when he said abruptly, 'Felix has been here, hasn't he?'

'Yes, as a matter of fact, he has,' I said.

'Is he still here?'

'No, he left this morning.'

'Are you sure?'

'Yes, I took him to the station myself, before the funeral. Why, Paul? What do you want him for?'

He gave me an embarrassed look, took a quick swallow of his drink, put the glass down, brought his hands together and cracked his knuckles. They were big, well-shaped hands,

88

but just then he looked as if he did not know what to do with them.

'Oh, I don't want him, I just wanted to find out if he was still around,' he said. 'Meg told me he was here, and of course we all know what kind of man he is and the problems you've had with him and so it seemed natural to wonder . . . Well, I mean, if he *had* been here while we were all at the funeral, it seemed just a possibility . . . Not as likely as its being the Bodwells, of course, who took those damned things, but still something to consider. Only we didn't want to say anything about it to the police, because we didn't want to make problems for you, if you see what I mean. You could just talk to him, we thought, and find out the facts.'

'How very kind.' I could not keep irony out of my voice, though in fact it really was kind of them. 'But no one ever found out any reliable facts by talking to Felix. However, as I said, I took him to the station before the funeral, so if the miniatures didn't disappear until after that, you can be sure he didn't steal them.'

He cracked his knuckles again. His walk through the windy evening had brought bright colour into his cheeks and ruffled his dark hair. He looked very young and strong and healthy.

'That's that, then,' he said. 'I hope you don't mind my asking you about it like this. I didn't want to do it, but Imogen said someone must, because after all he was far more likely to know the value of the things than people like the Bodwells, who seem to have been perfectly honest all the time they worked for Aunt Evelyn, which is about a year now. Not that Imogen is so sure about them being honest. She says they could easily have been helping themselves to a good deal more than their wages without anyone realizing it. But you know what Imogen's like when she's angry. She has to blame everything on someone, and she's terribly angry now, because of there being no money. Meg says she's sure the Bodwells never stole anything—I mean, before today—although she admits they might have cooked the housekeeping accounts without her spotting it. She just doesn't think they did. I like Meg, don't you? There's something about her . . . I don't know how to put it . . . Something that gets you, anyway. I never noticed it before, though we've met several times. Perhaps it's just something in the atmosphere of a day like this that brings out people's qualities. What do you think?'

'Oh, I'm sure you're right,' I answered gravely. Certainly the day had brought out certain qualities in Paul that I had never been aware of before. This edgy talkativeness seemed quite unlike him.

'I expect you think I'm a fool,' he said.

'Why should I think that?' I asked.

'About Meg. The way I've suddenly fallen

for her.'

'It's a thing that happens to people,' I said.

'But in this case . . . Well, she's crazy about Patrick, anyone can see that. So I'm wasting my time here.'

'You could always compete. She may find a passion for Patrick a bit unrewarding.'

'Because of Imogen, d'you mean?'

I had not expected him to go quite so directly to the point, but after hesitating a moment, I nodded.

'But I don't know if that means much,' I said. 'There's something between them and I think Meg takes it very seriously, but you know what they're both like. Rather like one another. They may forget all about one another as soon as they both go home.'

'So then Patrick might start stringing Meg along again, just for the hell of it.'

I looked at him uneasily. 'Does this really mean a great deal to you, Paul?'

He shrugged his shoulders, trying to look as if it did not.

'Perhaps I'll forget about it too when I go home,' he said. 'Anyway, I can't stay around to compete, I've a job to do. They gave me some time off for the funeral, but I can't stay here indefinitely. So I'd better see what I can do about forgetting, hadn't I? Unless there's a chance that Patrick and Imogen are serious about one another. Do you think that's possible? They've known each other for years and I've never seen much sign of them caring about each other until recently.'

'But they're both past their first youth, aren't they? They might be feeling like settling down.'

'Do you mean they might actually marry?' He looked incredulous.

'Stranger things have happened,' I said. 'Now that you mention it, I think they might suit each other very well.'

'The question is, do they realize that themselves?' He gave a sudden laugh. 'Imogen dwindling into a wife—that's something to think about, isn't it? But now that she's discovered she isn't going to inherit lots of money, perhaps marriage will seem more attractive than it used to.' He gulped down the rest of his drink. 'But I really didn't come to talk about these things and myself. I just wanted to find out if Felix was still here.'

'You haven't actually talked about yourself a great deal,' I said. I did not want to get back to talking about Felix. 'But I know what I'd do if I were you and you want Meg. She talked to me about looking for a new job in London, so I'd work at persuading her that that's a very good idea.'

He frowned. 'I don't want to catch her on the rebound. That's a recipe for trouble.'

'But getting her to London would be a first step, wouldn't it? After that there'd be no need to rush things. You could just wait and be nice to her while she's getting over Patrick.'

'Yes, I see. I suppose that's sense, if she'll listen to me. Well, thank you for letting me talk.' He stood up. 'And you don't mind what I said about Felix?'

'A very natural thing to ask, I'm afraid.'

I had my boiled egg presently and went to bed early, but I had a restless night. The wind was noisy and kept waking me and when I had been wakened my thoughts started to go round and round and kept me from falling asleep again. They kept worrying at the problem of what had really brought Felix to Allingford. I had never had much faith in his story of a customer in the neighbourhood for one of his dubious second-hand cars, since Allingford was rather far off his beat, or in his sudden desire for my company either. It was true that he had come to see me two or three times during the five years—since we had separated, just as he had this time, without warning and without any obvious reason for wanting to see me. But now that I knew that he had some relationship with the Bodwells, it looked after all fairly certain that that was what had brought him and that if he was not directly responsible for the theft of the miniatures, he was somehow involved in it. But if he was, what was I to do about it?

Let him get away with it? Wait for the police to catch him? Even drop a hint that would lead them to him, then wait for him to be tried and sent to prison?

Somehow he had always avoided prison until now and I could not see myself being the person who would lead him there. Anyway, wives did not have to give evidence against their husbands, did they? But could I simply do nothing?

I had to go to the clinic again next day and had one of my more difficult patients to deal with, who could not understand why I could not cure her of all her aches and pains although she was seventy-five and severely arthritic. Usually I felt very sorry for her and did my best to boost her morale, since that was really all that I could do for her, but that day I simply did not answer when she complained to me and I could feel myself looking at her with a kind of malevolence, as if she was wantonly imposing her afflictions on me, just to annoy me. I was absent-minded and snappish with everyone and when five o'clock came did not linger to talk to anyone, but left the place as quickly as possible.

I did not drive home but to the station and bought a ticket to Paddington. The journey from Allingford, on a good train, took fifty minutes and I was lucky enough to have to wait only ten minutes for one to come in. At Paddington I took a taxi and arrived in Little Carbery Street at about a quarter to seven. I knew there was a fair chance that Felix would not be at home, but if he was not I knew of several places where it might be worth my while to look for him. Anyway, I felt that I was doing something and that eased my tension. I paid off the taxi, turned to the door, pushed it open and started to climb the stairs inside.

As they had always been, they were very shabby. The house was narrow-fronted and Georgian, in a street that had once been two dignified terraces, facing each other, but which now consisted almost entirely of tall office buildings and blocks of flats. Only a few of the old houses remained, waiting to be torn down by the developers, who had devastated it far more effectively than the bombs of wartime, which had begun the destruction.

Our flat—it caught me by surprise to realize that that was what I still called it in my mind— was on the second floor. Toiling up the steep, seedy staircase, I reached the door and rang the bell beside it.

Immediately I heard footsteps inside, but they were not Felix's. The sound was made by high heels and it was a woman who opened the door. It took me a moment to recognize her as Mrs Bodwell. Her grey hair had turned auburn, the clever make-up on her face took at least ten years off her age and instead of the rusty black in which I had always seen her, she was wearing a well-cut trouser suit of emerald green. She had long, spectacular earrings of black and gold and they swung as she took a quick step back from the door, as if she thought that she could avoid me.

But she seemed to regret that movement of retreat, for she checked it and gave me a sardonic smile.

'I was afraid of this,' she said, 'but I never thought you'd get here so quickly.'

CHAPTER FIVE

'May I come in?' I said.

She hesitated, shrugged her shoulders, then stood aside for me to enter.

Her manner was totally different from that of the Mrs Bodwell I had known. No one could ever have taken this casual, rather haughty woman for a servant. If she had lost a good deal of her former quiet dignity, she had gained very much in self-assurance. She let me go ahead of her into the living-room, a long, panelled room with two tall windows, a high ceiling and a delicately carved marble fireplace. Felix had looked after the place well and the room was better furnished than when I had lived here with him.

'Are you living here?' I asked.

'Staying, just for the present,' Mrs Bodwell answered. 'Felix is very kindly putting us up till we find another job.'

'The same kind of job as the last?'

'Why not? It's what we do best and we can be together. That means a good deal to us. We've had to spend enough of our lives apart.'

'Will you be recommended again by Sir Oswald Smith-Ogilvie?'

She gave her sardonic smile again. She had not sat down, but was standing leaning with one elbow on the marble mantelpiece. Her auburn hair, I had realized by now, was a wig.

'So you've heard about that,' she said. For the first time her voice had a familiar sound, flat and toneless. 'Yes, I expect he'll help out. He's a good friend, is Felix.'

'The question is,' I said, 'do I tell the police where to find you? Even Sir Oswald won't be able to help much if I do that.'

'The police?' she said, lifting her darkened eyebrows. 'Why should they want us?'

'Look, there's no need to pretend,' I said. 'Everyone knows you took the miniatures. But if you're sensible about it, we might be able to come to some arrangement that would keep you out of trouble.'

'Miniatures?' she said. 'I don't know what you're talking about.'

'Oh, don't be a fool!' I said with irritation. 'Have you disposed of them already, because if you have there isn't much I can do about it, but if you've still got them somewhere around, I can probably put things straight for you and for Felix too.'

She shook her head so that her long earrings swung again.

'I honestly don't know what you're talking about,' she said. 'Do you mean those little pictures in the drawing-room?'

'Of course I mean those little pictures.'

'But what's happened to them?'

'They vanished at the same time as you. Are you going to tell me that's a coincidence?'

'Vanished?' she said. 'Stolen?'

'For God's sake, Mrs Bodwell, let's not waste time!' I said. 'I don't want to stay here any longer than I need and you don't want me here. And I don't care about you and your husband and what you did. I came merely because I want to keep Felix out of trouble. I don't know why I should mind about it, but for some reason I do. And if you feel you owe him anything, as you seem to, you'll talk sensibly now and the first thing is to stop pretending you didn't take the miniatures.'

She drew a finger along her jawbone, looking at me with a thoughtful frown, then remarked irrelevantly, 'My name's Rita.'

'All right, Rita,' I said. 'Where have you got them?'

She gave a sigh.

'The thing to do, it seems to me,' she said, 'is to go along and talk about all this with Jim and Felix. They're in the Waggoners, having a drink, and they won't be long, but if you're in a hurry, as you say, the best thing would be to go along and join them. I wouldn't like to go into a matter like this without them knowing. And perhaps you'll take more notice of what they say than you will of me.'

If she thought that three people telling me lies would make more impression than only one, she was probably right. Sheer weight of numbers might confuse me. But it was clear that she was not going to tell me anything

99

without consulting Jim and Felix, so it was probably best to get ahead with that.

I stood up. 'All right, let's go.'

I was really glad to get away from that room. It was assaulting me as I sat there with too many memories that I wanted to forget, of happiness, desperation, resignation. The load of emotion was a little too much to be borne. If I stayed there much longer, I thought, it might numb me into helplessness and acceptance. I walked out quickly, escaping from the charm and the threat and the sadness of the place.

The Waggoners was a pub to which I had often gone with Felix. It was only a few minutes' walk away from the flat, a small place, usually crowded, with a few high-backed settles and tables and generally a throng around the bar of people who knew one another and looked with a marked lack of welcome at any unfamiliar face. Felix and Jim Bodwell were among these, chattering happily, each nursing a mug of beer. When they saw me come in with Rita Bodwell they detached themselves from the crowd and without showing much surprise at seeing me, led us to a table in a corner, brought Rita a gin and tonic and me a glass of sherry. Pretty terrible sherry, I discovered, as it usually is in pubs, but that did not seem to matter. I did not want to slip accidentally into geniality or enjoyment of the evening.

Felix sat down beside me and put an arm round my shoulders.

'Well, this is nice,' he said. 'But I suppose there's a reason for it, not just a simple desire for our company.'

I removed his arm.

'The miniatures,' I said. 'I spent most of last night thinking about what I ought to do and I came to the conclusion that if you'd return them I'd do my best to see the family doesn't bring any charges. They were left to Nigel, so I suppose it would ultimately be his decision, but I don't think he's a vindictive person. But you've got to give them back. If you don't, I'll tell the police everything I know.'

There was a moment of silence round our table, then Rita said, 'She's been going on about this ever since she arrived, threatening to stir up trouble for us. I thought we'd all best get together and talk it over.'

'Yes,' Felix said thoughtfully. 'Yes, indeed.' He drank a little of his beer. 'Suppose you begin at the beginning, Virginia, and tell us what's happened to upset you.'

'As if you didn't know!' I said. 'The miniatures vanished. The Bodwells vanished. You vanished—after saying to me only the day before that the miniatures were the only valuable things in the house. Whether you actually stole them yourself or left it to the Bodwells I don't know. I took you to the station yesterday morning, but I didn't see you actually get on the train. I left you at the booking-office and when I left you there you could easily have taken a taxi up to the house, knowing it would be empty with everyone at the funeral, and grabbed the collection. But I suppose it's more probable that the Bodwells did the job and then joined you here, and I'll help you put things right if I can, but I'm not going to let you treat my friends like that. They've guessed already that you'd something to do with it, but they've said nothing about it to the police for my sake, which is extremely good of them, but I don't mean to let you take advantage of it.'

'Now wait,' Felix said while the two Bodwells looked at me woodenly. 'Someone's stolen the miniatures, is that it?'

'As if you didn't know—'

'Wait!' he interrupted. 'Just answer yes or no. I want to get a clear picture of the situation. The miniatures have been stolen?'

'Yes.'

'During the funeral?'

'Yes.'

'And because the Bodwells happened to decide to leave during the funeral, they're suspected of the theft?'

'Of course.'

'And somehow you've deduced that I was involved in it with them and you tracked them down to the flat. How did you do that?'

'As soon as I heard they'd got the job with

Mrs Arliss with a reference from Sir Oswald Smith-Ogilvie, I knew where to look.'

'I see, I see. And you've naturally taken a completely uncharitable view of their behaviour. You didn't think they could have any reason for leaving the house except to get away from the police.'

'It strikes me as unlikely. To leave suddenly like that without any warning, not leaving even a letter behind, or any lunch for anybody—isn't that highly suspicious?'

'Ah, no funeral baked meats.' Felix nodded his head as if now he understood my attitude. 'Very tiresome for everyone. Well, I wonder . . .' He looked at the Bodwells. 'Would it be best to explain to her why you really left?'

They exchanged glances, but said nothing.

'I know her, you know,' Felix said. 'Once she gets her teeth into a thing, she won't let go.'

'Go on then,' Rita said, 'but I don't like it. I don't like any of it. We haven't done anything wrong. And we can't give her the bloody miniatures, can we?'

'Well, no,' Felix agreed.

'Go on,' Jim said. 'As things are, we've nothing to lose by it.'

'Have some more sherry,' Felix said to me.

'No, thank you,' I answered.

He sipped his beer again. As usual, the level of it was descending very slowly in his mug.

'About leaving no lunch—' he began.

'That isn't important!' I exclaimed.

103

'Ah, but it is, it's very important,' he said. 'They'd never have done such a thing if they hadn't been in a great hurry. The fact is, they really can't afford to have any contact with the police. People in their position are never given a fair chance by the police. They've both got form, you see.'

'That means they've been in prison, doesn't it? I guessed that, more or less.' It was what I had made of Rita's remark that she and her husband had spent too much of their lives apart.

'Yes, of course, and that's why they needed a reference from me,' Felix said. 'They wanted to make a fresh start, and believe it or not, they've gone absolutely straight since they got out. However, their last employer happens to be dead. Suicide. A very sad business. So they couldn't ask him to help them. Anyhow, even if he'd been alive, I doubt if he'd have done anything for them. But they happen to be old friends of mine—I remember we met years ago here in the Waggoners—so I thought the least I could do was help them to a decent job. I was so glad it could be with Mrs Arliss, because I knew they'd get along splendidly. She'd never think of prying into their private lives and I knew they'd make her last years comfortable. Which they did. You can't say they didn't, can you?'

'No,' I agreed. 'But what was it their former employer had against them. What had they stolen from him?'

'Nothing—nothing whatever!' Felix said with exasperation. 'You've got theft on the brain. No, you see, the unfortunate thing about him was that he was an alcoholic and he'd a bad habit of driving when he'd drunk more than he should and one day he knocked down a little girl and killed her. Personally, I think the parents were to blame. They should never have let a child of that age out alone. I think people like that ought to be prosecuted. But the poor man panicked and drove away, then afterwards it preyed on his mind because he blamed himself terribly for what he'd done and he broke down and confided everything to the Bodwells. Well, they didn't turn him in to the police, because they were attached to him and they didn't want to get him into trouble, but he felt so bad that one night he took a big overdose of sleeping pills, after writing to the police and confessing he'd killed the child and telling them he'd been paying the Bodwells for their silence. An appalling slander. But Jim got five years and Rita three, which was grossly unjust, because a letter from an alcoholic who's just taken a bottleful of barbiturates is hardly reliable evidence, is it?'

'Blackmail!' I said.

'I don't like that word,' Jim Bodwell said.

For the first time since I had known him, his face was ugly.

'I expect there was more evidence than just

105

that letter,' I said.

'Oh, of course the police cooked up something between them,' Felix said, 'but nothing that a sane man would have taken seriously.'

'But I still don't understand what this has got to do with the miniatures,' I said.

'It's quite simple,' Felix answered. 'They waited till everyone had left the house to start getting the lunch, then Rita happened to go into the drawing-room to make sure that everything was straight, and she saw the miniatures had gone. They'd been there only half an hour before, but now the wall was stripped bare. So she and Jim discussed what they ought to do and decided that with their record the best thing would be to disappear. So they packed up and left and as they'd nowhere else to go, they came to me. And now they're looking for another job, but until they find one they're very welcome to be my guests, because, as I told you, they're old friends, and in telling you all I have about them I'm trusting you not to make trouble for them and me, because they were always dead honest with Mrs Arliss and very good to her too.'

'We were,' Rita said sombrely, as if she now regretted the fact. 'We never touched a thing that wasn't ours. We'd made up our minds to go straight and we did. But now this bloody thing has to happen to us. I ask you, why? What have we done to deserve it?'

106

'Run away, for one thing,' I said. 'In the circumstances it would have been far wiser to stay on the spot and report the theft to the police yourselves.'

She shook her head. 'You don't know anything. If a thing goes missing, the servants are the first people to be suspected. And in our situation our story would never have been believed, any more than you believe it. You don't believe it, do you?'

'Well, no,' I said.

'There you are, you see. No, we thought the thing was to clear out. We didn't reckon on being found so quickly. That business about Sir Oswald, it might never have come out, then you'd never have thought of looking for us here. Now I suppose we'll have to move on, because we can't return any miniatures we haven't got and you'll go to the police and that'll be the end of us.'

'Only you won't really go to them, will you?' Felix said, putting an arm round me again. 'I know you don't trust me an inch, but there's no reason why you should take that out on the Bodwells, who are absolutely blameless.'

'Except that they're a pair of callous blackmailers,' I said. 'Making money out of the death of a child—how can you go any lower than that?'

'I've told you I don't like that word,' Jim growled. 'You could find it dangerous, throwing it about like that.'

Felix turned on him. 'Don't threaten her. That isn't the way to manage her. She's a nice girl, you'll find, if you get to know her well, and the thing to do is to appeal to her sense of reason. Persuade her she's got no evidence that any of us knows anything about the disappearance of the miniatures, then she'll keep her promise and not make trouble for us.'

'And just how are you going to persuade her when her mind's made up already?' Rita asked.

'Think about who really took them,' Felix said.

She gave a scornful laugh. 'It could be anyone in that family. They're all crazy about money and they're all crazy too at finding there isn't any. And Huddleston's as bad as the rest of them. He thought he was going to get a rich wife. The only one I wouldn't suspect is little Meg. She's a decent enough child.'

'I haven't seen any signs that Paul cares so very much about money,' I said. 'I think he just cares for Meg.'

'Well, he's young,' she said, as if that explained an eccentricity in him. 'The young aren't realistic.'

'And Meg only cares about Huddleston,' Felix said, 'and he cares about Imogen, and she's never cared about anyone in her life. It's a sad story.'

'I didn't say he cares about her,' Rita said. 'I

just said he'd an idea he might marry her as she was coming into money. But that'll be off now, I shouldn't wonder.'

'D'you think they were actually getting near to marriage, if they'd enough money between them?' Felix asked.

'Oh, yes,' she said. 'Being a servant, you know, one hears things.'

'But what's all this got to do with the miniatures?' I demanded again, feeling that I was being deliberately led away from the subject and that if I let this continue it would become harder and harder to bring it back.

'Isn't it obvious?' Felix said. 'You said they were left to Nigel, so it's hardly likely he'd steal them, and you don't think Paul's avaricious, though of course you can't possibly be certain about that, but you do know Imogen's pretty desperate for money. We saw that the other day when she came to see you. So suppose the truth is that at last Imogen really wants to marry and she knows she won't get Huddleston without money. So she helps herself to the only moderately valuable asset in the house and hides it somewhere till she can dispose of it. And that means the miniatures are probably still in the house and if you can organize a search, you'll turn them up.'

'Unless Huddleston's already disposed of them for her,' Jim suggested. 'They might be in it together. Then you won't find them.'

I stood up.

'I think I've had enough of this,' I said. 'It's all nonsense. You're just doing your best to confuse me. But if the miniatures are found tied up in a nice parcel on Mrs Arliss's doorstep in the morning, I won't say anything to anybody about what I know. But if they aren't there, I'm going to the police. I mean it. Now I'm going home.'

I slid out from behind the table and set off to look for a taxi.

I had some fish and chips in the cafeteria at Paddington, then took the next train to Allingford. In London, between the tall houses, I had hardly noticed the storm that was building up, but at Allingford, when I came out of the station and went towards where I had parked my car, the wind gave me a buffet that almost sent me reeling. It whipped dust into my eyes and sent torn scraps of newspaper fluttering wildly along the road.

It was about half past ten when I reached home. The windows were rattling and the chimneys moaning. The one tree in the garden, a tall birch, swept its branches against the roof so forcefully that I wondered how many tiles I should find had fallen down in the morning. But I went to bed almost at once. My mind was foggy with weariness and full of uncertainty about what I had been told that evening. It was only after I had gone to bed, feeling that I should be asleep in a few minutes, that my thoughts cleared abruptly, leaving me even more wakeful than I had been the night before.

I thought mainly of Felix, feeling the depression that I always did after any meeting with him. It was always so tempting to believe what he said. It promised such comfort and peace. I was sure that if only I could convince myself that he had told me the truth that evening and that neither he nor the Bodwells had had anything to do with the theft of the miniatures, I should go to sleep like a child. I began to want sleep with a kind of frenzy, feeling that perhaps I had somehow lost the trick of it and would stay awake for ever.

One of my problems was that I knew that Felix was always very loyal to his friends. They might be utterly contemptible people, descending to such depths as blackmail, which I was sure that he had never sunk to himself, but still if they were in trouble he regarded it as simply a normal thing to do to stand up for them staunchly. His test of a friend seemed to be merely that he should show some signs of liking Felix. That was all that he demanded of him. He was always touchingly grateful for being liked. It had seemed to me one of his more attractive, though at times also one of his most maddening qualities. It was all part of the moral confusion in which he found himself so perfectly at home.

But suppose he was right that it was Imogen who had stolen the miniatures . . .

He was shrewd in his way and he knew her fairly well. However, she was not one of the people who passed his test of friendship. She did not like him at all. So he would have no conscience about trying to blacken her character, even if he did not believe a word that he was saying against her, and he knew that if he could convince me that she was the thief I would not go to the police about the Bodwells.

Indeed, I realized, I was unlikely to go to them about Imogen. I did not really care much who ended up in possession of the miniatures, and if she had taken them, it was, it seemed to me, a family matter between her and Nigel and they could fight it out without interference from me. The thought that bothered me deeply and kept me awake was that by keeping silent about the connection between the Bodwells and Felix, I was acting as an accomplice and was almost as responsible for the theft as they probably were.

But suppose he had spoken the truth . . He sometimes did.

There I was, back to the beginning again and as wide awake as ever.

Gazing upwards into the darkness, I began to worry away at the old problem of what my life would have been like if I had never met Felix. A fruitless question, but one that I had never been able to put entirely behind me. Would I perhaps have remained a hard-working spinster, not unhappy, but feeling restlessly at certain times that I had missed something? Or would I have married some honest, responsible man whom I could have loved steadily and uncritically and grown old with in peace? Or would I simply have made some other mistake, as bad as or worse than the mistake of marrying Felix? Some people are disaster prone when it comes to marriage. Was I one of those, I wondered, and had I really come out of things not as badly as I might?

I had met Felix at a party when I was staying for a weekend with a friend in London. He had telephoned me next day and taken me out to dinner that evening. The friend whom I was staying with had encouraged it. She had said that we would be good for one another. I never found out how much she knew about Felix. That was the first occasion when I heard the story of his having crossed the Greenland ice-cap on skis. I suppose he had recently met someone who had really done it, or he had read some book about it. It never occurred to me to doubt a word of what he told me and I found it enthralling. Other stories followed. They were all graphically but modestly told and there was something so gentle and considerate about him, so surprisingly intuitive for a man whose life had been filled with so much action, that before I knew where I was, I was in love with him. His looks, of course, had something to do with it. I loved to watch his mobile, triangular face with the brilliantly blue eyes hooded by his drooping eyelids. There had really been nothing surprising in the fact that I had soon wanted to marry him.

What had been truly surprising, what surprised me still when I thought about it, had been that he had wanted to marry me. I had wondered sometimes if he had been in a mood of wanting to achieve some stability in his life and had thought that I could give it to him. If that had been so, then he had made as much of a mistake about me as I had about him, for what he had perhaps taken for stability had been nothing but a kind of shyness, which, as it happened, I had been longing to shed. Hidden by it, I had had a stormy temper, a jealous disposition and a longing for adventure. The kind of adventure that he had told me about, not the kind that he actually provided later. And I had had very little insight into my own nature. I had never expected at that time to have to think out for myself what values were sufficiently important to me to let my marriage go to wreck on them. I had thought that that was the kind of thing that one knew all about without working at it and that someone one loved would automatically turn out to be faultless. So when it had come to supplying the kind of understanding for which Felix may have been briefly searching, I had been a total failure.

The wind gained in force throughout the earlier part of the night, while rain lashed the windows, then at last it began to abate. As it grew quieter the turmoil in my brain abated somewhat too. For a time I more or less convinced myself that the right thing for me to do next day, if the miniatures had not been returned, which of course they would not have been, was to tell Patrick about the connection between Felix and the Bodwells, then leave it to him to decide what steps ought to be taken next. But Felix had succeeded in planting a doubt of Patrick in my mind. The faint possibility that he and Imogen between them had stolen the miniatures made me think how ridiculous it would be to hand Felix and the Bodwells over to him as scapegoats. Yet the thought of going to the police myself without even consulting anyone else made me toss and turn in my bed in sheer dread. I tried to assure myself that there was nothing to worry about, because Felix would have the sense to see that the miniatures were returned by the morning, then again I was sure he would not. Sooner or later I would have to make up my mind what to do. There was no escaping it.

Then all at once I knew what I was going to do. I would tell the whole story to Nigel. The miniatures, after all, were his property, so he was more concerned with the matter than anyone else and less likely to be involved in the theft, and at the same time he was a cautious, thoughtful man who would not act on an angry impulse. We would be able to talk the situation over coolly and decide between us what he ought to do. I was not sure what I hoped to achieve by this, since in the end someone was going to have to talk to the police, but at least the decision gave me the feeling that responsibility would be shared. I fell asleep soon after I had arrived at it and did not wake until eight o'clock.

The morning was grey and still. Going downstairs in the dressing-gown that had offended Felix, I saw lilac blossoms, shredded by the wind, scattered on my lawn, which was sodden with rain. But everything was motionless now.

I had coffee and my usual piece of toast, then got dressed, got my car out of the garage and drove through the town to the Arliss house. I found an elm tree had crashed across the drive half way up it. The tree had been rotten with Dutch elm disease and had been doomed anyway, but it was a sad sight to see it with its roots in the air and a gaping hole where they had been torn out of the earth. The gravel of the drive was blotched with puddles. I stopped my car and got out, walked around the fallen tree and picked my way between the puddles to the house.

Even in that short distance I got my shoes muddy. Of course there was no parcel of miniatures on the doorstep. I had not expected that there would be and hardly gave a thought to the possibility that they had already been found and taken inside. All the same, the fact depressed me. In the light of morning my visit to Felix seemed utterly irrational. All that it had done was warn the Bodwells of how easily they could be found, so that by now they would have left his flat and gone into hiding somewhere else.

When I rang the bell it was Nigel who opened the door. He was wearing his usual double-breasted dark suit and his black tie. His long cheeks glistened faintly from recent shaving. He gave me a solemn smile and said, 'Ah, Virginia. Good morning. What a night we've had, eh? And that tree down. It crashed in the evening. It made quite an alarming noise. Everyone was out but me. I must get in touch with someone, I suppose, to come and chop it up and remove it. Do you know anyone in the neighbourhood who tackles that kind of job? It's not the kind of thing I know anything about. Perhaps we could find someone in the Yellow Pages.'

He had ushered me into the house and closed the door behind me.

I told him of a firm of landscape gardeners who had removed a tree for me that had been growing too big for my small garden and he took a notebook and pencil out of his breast pocket and wrote down their name.

Then he said, 'You've come to see Imogen, I

expect. She's still in bed. I don't think she ever gets up much before midday. I was thinking of going back to Oxford today, but of course I can't get my car down the drive now. I might go back by train, I suppose, and come back and collect the car when the tree's been dealt with, but that may take days. I really don't know what to do.'

'Yes, it's difficult, isn't it?' I agreed. 'But if you don't want to get away in a hurry, I'd like to talk to you. It was you I came to see, not Imogen. It's about the miniatures.' I hesitated. 'You haven't heard anything about them, I suppose.'

'Not a thing, I'm afraid, but I expect the police will find them sooner or later,' he said, not sounding too concerned. 'Things like that aren't easy to dispose of. Art thefts are more difficult than the thieves often realize. Of course, the miniatures aren't highly valuable and if they were quietly sold off one by one I dare say it might be managed without attracting attention. All the same, I can't see the Bodwells as experienced art thieves. I imagine they acted on impulse when they took the collection and will very likely abandon it somewhere when they discover the risks of getting rid of it. In any case, I don't mean to let myself be too upset by the affair. It was a kind thought of Aunt Evelyn's to leave it to me, which she did, I imagine, because she recognized I was the one member of the family with any appreciation of such things, but I wasn't expecting it, so the disappointment of losing it isn't as great as it might be.'

'But you see, I've found out where the Bodwells are,' I said, 'and I'd like to talk that over with you.'

'Oh?' he said, looking at me rather blankly. 'Do you mean you found that out by yourself? How extraordinary. However did you manage it? But come into the drawing-room and tell me about it. I find this most intriguing, since the police don't seem to know where to look.'

He threw the door of the drawing-room open.

I believe I screamed. Somebody did. I heard it and it was not Nigel. I had no awareness of screaming, but only heard it and felt the shock of seeing Imogen on the floor in the middle of the room with blood matting her hair and clotted darkly down one side of her face. Her eyes were staring. Her dead face was grey-white. There was blood on her hands, which were flung wide, and splashes of it on her dress, the dress that she had worn the day before, and on the carpet. Her body had a look of heavy rigidity, as if she had lain there for several hours.

The miniatures were back on the wall.

CHAPTER SIX

Nigel remained sedate. He walked past me to within about a yard of Imogen's body, stood still there, staring down, then turned, as I thought, towards the telephone. But it was for the door that he was making, to turn off the light switch beside it. It was only as he did so that I became aware that the light had been on when we came into the room, a pale yellow gleam in the daylight.

'You oughtn't to have done that,' I said. 'We ought to have left things exactly as we found them.'

'You're quite right.' His voice was much steadier than mine. 'It was automatic, but of course a mistake. To turn it on again, however, wouldn't put it right. I'll leave it as it is. We can tell the police it was on when we came in. Don't you think that's best?'

'Are you going to telephone the police now?' I asked.

'Unless you'd prefer to do it yourself.'

'No, no, you do it.'

He picked up the telephone, dialled, gave his name and address to someone who answered and said that he wished to report a murder. He sounded fantastically matter-of-fact.

Someone replied to him, to whom he said,

'Oh, indubitably. No one commits suicide or dies by accident by hitting herself over the head with a copper coal shovel. The victim, I should have said, is Miss Imogen Dale, the niece of Mrs Evelyn Arliss, who, as you may know, died recently . . . Yes, I should say Miss Dale has been dead for several hours, but a friend and I have only just discovered her body . . . You will? Thank you. Then we'll expect you.'

He put the telephone down again.

Until he mentioned it, I had not taken in the fact that there was a heavy, antique copper coal scoop lying on the floor near to where Imogen lay. I had often seen it before, thrust into the coal in the copper coal scuttle that stood at one side of the fireplace. It ought to have caught my attention at once, but like the light which I had not noticed was on, it had not struck me as strange that it should be there.

I seemed to be past noticing anything but Imogen herself and I could hardly bear to look at her. A dark haze seemed to fill the room. I felt frozen where I was, longing to leave it, but unable to move. Nigel was coping with the emergency far better than I was. But then, as he had said, he had had plenty of experience of violent death during the war. It was natural death that he found awesome.

'That's strange,' he observed.

He had been walking slowly round the room and was standing now at the french window.

'I remember perfectly well I bolted it last night,' he said. 'Top and bottom. I went round the house before I went up to my room, as I usually do at home, and made sure that all the windows and the back door were bolted. I didn't bolt the front door, because everyone else was out, but I'm certain about this one. And now it's unbolted.'

'I suppose because the murderer left that way.' My voice was much higher than usual and did not feel as if it belonged to me.

'Or wanted us to think that he did. One or the other. Imogen herself would hardly have opened it to go out into the garden on a night like last night. We must point it out to the police when they get here.'

I suddenly felt intensely angry with Nigel for being so composed, so much his normal self when I was feeling that I had no self which I could trust to behave in any reasonable way. I might have said something stupid and regrettable if the doorbell had not rung just then.

'There they are,' I said and, feeling a kind of release from the immobility that had kept me helpless, turned quickly to answer it.

'Amazingly prompt,' Nigel said as I went. 'Admirably efficient. I'm surprised.'

However, it was not the police. It was Patrick Huddleston, wearing one of his flowery shirts again and the cheerfullest of smiles on his face.

'Virginia!' he exclaimed, as if it were astonishing but perfectly delightful to find me there. He seemed to be overflowing with high spirits, some of which he lavishly expended on me. 'Of course I've only come about my car. Imogen isn't up yet, I imagine, or is she, just for once? Have you seen her? Has she told you anything? Naturally I realize I can't move the car yet, but I thought I'd find out if they've made any plans about the tree, because if it's going to be some time before it's moved, I'll have to hire a car. It's nothing to worry about, I just wanted to know how things stand. And to see Imogen, if possible.'

I could make nothing of it and his cheerfulness was peculiarly upsetting. I felt like shrieking.

His voice changed abruptly. 'What's wrong, Virginia? Are you ill?'

'Come inside,' I said. 'I don't understand about the car, but—well, come inside.'

'It's only that it's in the garage here,' he said. 'Imogen told me to leave it there when the tree crashed and I couldn't get it away. What *is* wrong, Virginia?'

As he came in and I closed the door behind him, Nigel emerged from the drawing-room and I thought that there was no reason why he should not be the bearer of the bad news, instead of me. He accepted the responsibility solemnly, holding out a hand, which plainly took Patrick by surprise, for they had known each other far too long to be on hand-shaking terms. He took the hand, but his eyebrows went up.

'An appalling thing has happened, Patrick,' Nigel said in his wooden way, sounding as if nothing had ever appalled him very deeply. 'I can hardly bring myself to speak about it, but it seems only right to prepare you. I know you were very attached to Imogen—'

'What the hell?' Patrick said explosively, pushed past Nigel and strode into the drawing-room.

It was perhaps cowardly, but Nigel and I stayed where we were, looking at one another. We listened, but there was no sound from the room. Then at last Patrick reappeared in the doorway. His colour had drained away, leaving his tanned face a sallow grey. His dark eyes were glazed with shock.

'You've called the police, of course,' he said in a level voice.

'Of course,' Nigel said.

'When did you discover it?'

'A few minutes ago. Virginia came to see me—something about the miniatures—we went into the drawing-room . . . Which reminds me, the miniatures have been returned. Odd that that didn't register with me till this moment. Very strange, isn't it? But a trivial thing in the circumstances.'

'They were there when Imogen and I got back here last night,' Patrick said. 'We had

124

dinner together at the Rose and Crown, then I drove her home and I came in and we talked for a little while and wondered about the miniatures and how they'd been returned and when. And then the tree crashed and I couldn't get my car away, so Imogen told me to put it into the garage. That's why I came this morning . . .' His voice dried up, like a trickle of water disappearing into sand. He had spoken with carefully controlled monotony, but with great concentration, as if putting effort into saying these relatively unimportant things offered some escape from the one important thing on his mind. 'We were going to get married, you know. We decided it yesterday evening.'

'My dear chap, that's terrible—terrible. I can't tell you how sorry . . .'

At that point Nigel had a fit of coughing, so that he really could not go on saying how sorry he felt, which was lucky for him, because marriage was a subject that had always tended to embarrass him. Sometimes he acted as if it were a great happiness mysteriously denied to him, and sometimes as if it could only be the concern of idiots.

Not that I was doing any better than he was, since I was struck dumb.

After a moment he went on, 'But were you and Imogen here when the tree came down, because I was under the impression that I was alone in the house? I knew you and she had

125

gone out to dinner and I thought Paul and Meg had gone to the cinema together and I hadn't heard anyone come in.'

'Where *are* Paul and Meg?' I asked. 'Does anyone know?'

'They went out shopping,' Nigel answered. 'The three of us had breakfast together, then they went down into the town to buy some groceries and so on. I should think they'll soon be back. But were you really here when the tree fell, Patrick? I didn't see you.'

'We didn't see you,' Patrick said.

'I didn't actually go out,' Nigel said. 'I could see what had happened from my window. It was quite dark already, of course—I think the time was about a quarter to eleven—but I could see the great gap in the trees. And I'd already undressed and put on my dressing-gown, so it really didn't seem worth while going out.'

'Imogen and I went,' Patrick said. 'And we saw at once I shouldn't be able to get my car away, so, as I said, we put it in the garage and I walked home. It wasn't a pleasant walk. It hadn't started to rain yet, but the wind was very violent.'

I was trying to think clearly about something that seemed important to me.

'How long were you in the house before the tree crashed?' I asked.

'Oh, not long,' Patrick said. 'Ten minutes, quarter of an hour, something like that. Why?

126

Does it matter?'

I thought it was possible that it mattered a great deal, but I did not want to explain why.

'And you're sure the miniatures were back on the wall?' I said.

'Oh yes, it was the first thing we noticed when we went into the room. We'd other things to talk about, as you can imagine, but it seemed so extraordinary, we just stood there and stared at them.'

'And that was about half past ten?'

He gave a frown, suddenly looking at me intently.

'What's on your mind, Virginia?'

What was on my mind was that if it was the Bodwells who had returned the miniatures, they must have moved extremely quickly after I left them in the Waggoners to have been able to hang them up in the drawing-room by half past ten.

But it was just possible. It had been about half past ten when I had reached home, having travelled back from London by train, but I had delayed for some time at Paddington while I ate my fish and chips. If the Bodwells had not delayed at all after I left them and had driven fast, they might conceivably just have managed to hang up the pictures before Imogen and Patrick came in. They would have been able to do most of the journey on the M4, having to slow up only in the narrow, winding roads about four miles from Allingford.

Getting into the house would have been no problem for them. They probably still had the keys that they had used while they were employed by Mrs Arliss, and Nigel had left the front door unbolted. And perhaps, I thought, they had just hung up the miniatures when they heard Imogen and Patrick come in by the front door, so had slipped quickly out of the drawing-room into the garden by the french window, naturally leaving it unbolted.

They would of course have left their car in the road, since they would not have risked drawing attention to themselves by driving up to the house in it, so even if they had lingered for some reason, they would not have been trapped by the fallen tree. And Imogen and Patrick, passing the car before turning in at the drive, would not have noticed it.

'What's on your mind?' Patrick repeated, beginning to sound angry now as well as suspicious. 'Why d'you keep on about those damned miniatures when Imogen . . . Oh God, Imogen!'

He turned and stalked back into the drawing-room.

Nigel gave a deep sigh.

'Poor fellow,' he said. 'To have made up their minds at last and then this . . . But shall I tell you what's on *my* mind, Virginia? Imogen was a big, strong woman and if anyone had attacked her she'd have fought and screamed. But I heard nothing. I was upstairs, quietly reading, and honestly I didn't hear a thing. Isn't that strange?'

'You didn't hear her and Patrick come in either,' I said. 'This house is very solidly built and the storm was noisy and would have drowned other sounds and perhaps you dozed off for a little.'

'Well, you may be right. I hope so. I was certainly very tired. The funeral and all—it was a difficult day. But all the same . . . You see, it could mean the poor woman was stunned before she could scream by someone she trusted. By one of us, that's what I'm trying to say. A terrible thought. But what do you think about it, Virginia? Is my imagination too lurid?'

The last person I would ever have thought of as having a lurid imagination, indeed, any imagination at all, was Nigel, but he was not a fool either. However, Meg and Paul, arriving home from the shops just then, made me forget his question for the time being.

They had to be told what had happened and they had barely taken it in, had taken only the briefest of horrified glances into the drawing-room from the doorway, when the police arrived. In the few minutes before they did Meg had dropped the basket of groceries that she was carrying, had pressed both hands to her mouth to hold in a scream, then had buried her face against Paul's chest. I could see that if his hands had not been full of packages, his arms would have gone round her, but before I could free him of what he was carrying, she had abruptly pushed him away, as if it had been he who had been trying to hold her, had picked up the basket that she had dropped and fled into the kitchen. I took Paul's packages from him and followed her.

She was moving about in a hurried, stumbling way, making a great show of putting her purchases tidily away, but suddenly she sat down at the table and clutched her head with both hands.

'I hated her, Virginia,' she said. '*I hated* her. When I found out what I did about her and Patrick, I could have killed her. I *thought* I could have killed her. But not really—not like this.'

'I shouldn't say that sort of thing to the police,' I said, 'even if they're used to people committing imaginary murders, as I believe they are.'

'Of course I won't,' she said, 'but you knew it, didn't you? So you'll tell them, I expect.'

'Why d'you think I should?'

'Because it's what I'd do if I were you.'

'I don't think you would really.'

'But who else has any motive?'

'Luckily I haven't got to work that one out,' I said. 'Nor have you. We don't really know much about Imogen's life, do we? It could be someone out of the past, perhaps someone who was jealous. You haven't heard, have you, that she and Patrick had decided to get married? You may not be the only person who hated her for that. Anyway, she was in trouble of some sort, I'm sure of that, and it may have caught up with her.'

She gave her head a slight shake as if she found everything that I had said irrelevant, then stood up and went on more soberly putting her tins and packets away.

When the police came they herded us all into the small morning-room, to keep us out of their way while they made their first inspection of Imogen's body and the drawing-room. There seemed to be a great many of them. One was the young sergeant who had come the day before when Patrick had reported the theft of the miniatures, but Inspector Roper had been replaced by a Detective-Superintendent Chance, a gaunt yet curiously flabby sort of man, whose footsteps seemed to drag and whose words came gratingly with a sound of great weariness. He looked as if he took a dislike to us all collectively, before telling us politely that he would like presently to question us one by one in the dining-room and that he was sorry that we might find our wait a long one.

When he had gone, Paul said, 'I suppose he's going to ask us all for our alibis.'

'I have none,' Nigel said. 'I was alone in my room the whole evening.'

'Paul and I were out together,' Meg said.

'We went to the cinema. I think it was soon after eleven when we got in. We went straight upstairs and—and said good-night and went to our rooms.'

Her slight hesitation over the saying of that good-night made it sound as if it might have been one that had taken them some time. I wondered if Meg, exposed to Paul's youth and good looks, was already getting over her feeling for Patrick, or if she was merely using Paul to distract herself from the pain of her emotions.

'And you, Virginia?' Patrick asked. His face was still haggard and sallow, but his eyes were alert.

'As a matter of fact, I went to London after I left the clinic,' I said. 'It was about half past ten when I got home.'

'London?' Nigel said incredulously, as if there were something extraordinarily eccentric about my having gone there. 'Good gracious me! I never go to London nowadays if I can avoid it. The noise, the traffic, the foreigners. And you can never get a taxi when you want one. Why did you go? No, I beg your pardon, it's not my business to ask.'

'I don't mind,' I said. 'I went to see Felix. There were some problems I wanted to talk over with him.'

'So the fact is,' Patrick said, 'none of us has an alibi, because the murder was almost certainly later than eleven. That's about when

132

I left and Imogen was alive then. And Meg and Paul must have come in only a few minutes later and it's hardly likely to have happened in that space of time. That's if you accept my statement that Imogen was alive when I left. No reason why you should, of course. Perhaps you don't.'

His voice had become monotonous again. He might have been speaking to himself. He had moved towards the window and was gazing out at the garden with a heavy frown on his face.

'My dear chap, don't talk like that,' Nigel said. 'In fact, I don't think any of us should be talking like this. We'll only get on each other's nerves. I wonder if we could have some tea. Meg, do you think you could make us some tea? I'm sure we should all appreciate it.'

Meg got up from the sofa where she had just sat down and went out to the kitchen.

But by the time that she returned with the tea-tray, Nigel had been summoned by the sergeant to the dining-room and by the time that he returned the tea was growing cold. He looked sombre and absent-minded. Meg was the next to be summoned, then Paul, then Patrick. I was last.

Waiting for my turn, I had noticed that as one by one they returned to the morning-room there was a curious new thoughtfulness about them. Silence fell on the little room. It was silence with an undercurrent of antagonism in it, as if at last we were becoming consciously suspicious of one another.

When I went into the dining-room I found Superintendent Chance seated at the long mahogany table. The sergeant seated himself at the far end of it, with a notebook open in front of him. A good many of the pages of the notebook had already been filled. He sat with a ballpoint pen poised over a blank page and an encouraging smile on his face.

I took the chair to which Mr Chance waved me, told him my name and address and that I was an old friend of Mrs Arliss and the family.

'And what brought you here this morning?' he asked.

I had had time, waiting for the others to be questioned, to work out an edited version of the truth about my recent actions.

'It was because of the miniatures,' I said. 'I was worried about them—the way they vanished, you know. You've been told about that, I'm sure. I came to ask Mr Tustin if he'd had any news about them.'

'Not knowing at the time that they'd already been returned?'

'No.'

'When did you find they had?'

'At the same time as I discovered Miss Dale's body.'

'And that was the only reason why you came here? To talk to Mr Tustin? You hadn't some thought in your mind of what might have happened to the miniatures?'

I shook my head. 'Except what we all thought, that the Bodwells had taken them.'

'Ah yes, the Bodwells.' He placed the tips of his fingers together. They were long, thin fingers with bony knuckles. 'It may interest you to know that we've identified the Bodwells from their fingerprints. A dangerous couple who took domestic posts, as they did here, picked up material for blackmail when they could and if there was none available, soon moved on, helping themselves when they went to minor valuables. They've both been in gaol more than once. But their behaviour here wasn't characteristic. It almost looks as if they intended to go straight after their last sentence, though the reference with which they got the job was a forgery. It was supposed to have been supplied by a Sir Oswald Smith-Ogilvie, but to the best of our knowledge, no such person exists.'

'Dear me,' I said. Then immediately I felt, because of the thoughtful look that he gave me, that this had been quite the wrong sort of thing to say. It would have been better to say nothing.

'It may even be that they really were going straight,' Mr Chance went on. 'They'd been here a year without apparently misappropriating anything. Miss Randall is fairly sure there was no fiddling of the housekeeping accounts and Mrs Arliss, from all I've heard, would hardly have been a promising prospect for blackmail. Her liking for a little flutter now and then wouldn't have given them much of a hold over her. So except for the disappearance of the miniatures, nothing suspicious happened while they were here. And now the strange way that the things have reappeared makes it look less likely than it did at first that the Bodwells ever took them. It strikes me as quite likely that they discovered the theft, panicked and bolted, knowing that with records like theirs they'd be suspected. What doesn't seem to me likely is that if they'd stolen the pictures, they'd ever have brought them back again.'

'No,' I said.

'But somebody stole the pictures, or at least removed them, then brought them back again. Have you any ideas of your own who it could have been?'

'Is it important?' I asked. 'I mean, compared with—the other thing that happened?'

'I believe you brought the subject up yourself,' he said. 'Didn't you say you came here this morning because you'd been thinking about them?'

'Yes, but that was before I knew anything about Miss Dale.'

'And if the two things are connected?'

'But the miniatures were returned before Miss Dale and Mr Huddleston went into the room last night,' I said. 'He's sure of that. So

136

the murder can't have had anything to do with Miss Dale finding out who the thief was. And even if she did, that would hardly be an adequate motive for murder, would it?'

'Perhaps not, but if I told you some of the things that make people kill, you'd be surprised. And there's a—shall we call it an oddity?—about the two events, coming so close together. Can you by any chance tell me if the pictures have been replaced in their original places?'

'I'm afraid I hardly glanced at them this morning. I was too shocked. But anyway, I never took enough notice of them to remember what their original places were.'

He nodded, the weary look on his face deepening. He was tired of me already.

'That's what everyone says. Only Mr Tustin seems to have had some interest in them. They're his property, of course, so that's natural, but even he isn't sure about their positions. To leave that subject for the present, however, am I right that you knew Miss Dale fairly well?'

'I've known her a long time,' I said, 'but I wouldn't say that I knew her specially well. We were always on friendly terms, but never really intimate.'

'Was she a rich woman?'

'She always talked as if she was short of money.'

'Plenty of rich people do.'

'Yes, but I know it was a great shock when she discovered she wasn't going to inherit any money from Mrs Arliss. She talked about having to sell her house and move into a flat.'

'Do you know where her money came from in the first place? She didn't work, did she?'

'No. I think she inherited a certain amount from her mother.'

'A sister of Mrs Arliss?'

'Yes.'

'Then wasn't she a pretty rich woman too?'

'Only moderately,' I said. 'The two sisters may have started out with about the same amount of money, but Mrs Arliss married a rich man and Mrs Dale a poor one, and the Dales had two children, Imogen and Jennifer, so that what was left was split in two, so there can't have been a great deal left for either of them.'

'This Jennifer Dale, she's the mother of Mr Goss, is she?'

'She was. She married a journalist—not a very successful one—then was killed in a car crash when Paul was still a boy. Then his father died of a coronary two or three years later and Paul went to live for a time with Imogen. She was very good to him.'

'A generous woman, then, even if she wasn't a rich one.'

'Generous to Paul, anyway.'

'Well liked in general?'

I was not sure of the answer to that, so I

said, 'I think so.'

'Not the sort of woman to make enemies?'

'I don't think so. But I didn't know much about her private life.'

'Did she ever speak to you as if she was afraid of anyone?'

I hesitated and he noticed it at once.

'She did?' he said.

'Not exactly,' I said. 'I was trying to remember just what she said to me. It was soon after she'd discovered she wasn't going to inherit any money from her aunt. She came to see me and she seemed so extremely upset I asked her if she was in any real trouble and she said it was nothing that you could call trouble, but I'd a feeling that wasn't true. Still, I'm sure she didn't say anything about being afraid of anyone.'

'Were you surprised when you heard she and Mr Huddleston had got engaged?'

'I don't think I really thought much about it. There was too much else to think about at the time.'

'Yes, of course.' He was looking at me, but vaguely, his eyes seeming to focus on something some way beyond me. 'Now there's just one more thing I want to ask you, then I'll leave you in peace. As a matter of routine, will you tell me where you were between, say, nine o'clock and midnight last night?'

'*Nine* o'clock?' I said. 'But wasn't she out to dinner with Mr Huddleston at the Rose and

Crown?'

'Probably,' he answered, 'but we haven't checked it yet and the medical evidence, the little we know at the moment, is, as always, uncertain.'

'Well, at nine o'clock I was in London,' I said. This was the part of the interview that I had been rehearsing at the back of my mind all the time that we had been talking. I had chosen and rejected half a dozen different ways of dealing with it. 'I left the Clinic—the Lane Clinic, where I work part-time—about five o'clock and took a train to Paddington. I wanted to see my husband. He was down here for a few days and we discussed the question of divorce. We've been separated for five years, but we never made up our minds to a divorce, I don't know why. But when he was leaving I promised him I'd think the matter over carefully and let him know how I felt. And of course, when I thought about it I could see how absurd it had been not to get things tidied up long ago, and I suddenly decided to go to London and tell him so. I know I could have telephoned, but I felt there'd be a good many things we'd have to discuss—how to go about the whole thing, I mean, getting lawyers and so on—and that it would be better if we talked it over, taking as long as we needed. So we met and settled things, then I went back to Paddington and had a snack there . . .'

I do not know why it was, but it was at that

point that I got the feeling that I had been talking too much. Why should I have volunteered so much about my private affairs unless it was that I was covering up something else? What I had been saying must have sounded as dreadfully rehearsed as in fact it was. There was something in the way that Mr Chance was looking at me that made me feel sure I had blundered. But there was nothing for me to do now but go on.

'It was about ten-fifteen when I got back to Allingford,' I said. 'I'd left my car at the station and drove home. It was ten-thirty when I got there. And from then on I was alone. I can't prove I didn't go out again.'

He nodded absently, as if he had stopped bothering about me, indeed had not bothered about me much from the beginning. Asking for Felix's address, which the sergeant wrote down, he added that there was no reason why I should not go home now if I wanted to.

I wanted to very much, but first I went back to the morning-room, where I found that the others had reached the stage of sandwiches and coffee, and asked if I could help in any way if I stayed. Nobody seemed to want me, so I went out to my car, which I had some difficulty backing down the drive, because of all the police cars that were parked there, but eventually I edged my way out into the road and set off for Ellsworthy Street.

For a little while there was a sense of relief

simply at being alone in my car until I suddenly realized that I was driving recklessly and had nearly knocked over a cyclist. After that I drove at a snail's pace and the shock and distress of the morning abruptly hit me. Leaving the car in the street I went into the house and went straight to the telephone.

I dialled Felix's number. It rang and rang and nobody answered. But just as I was going to give up, wondering what on earth I should do next, I heard Felix's voice.

'Oh, it's you, Virginia,' he said as soon as I started to speak. 'I had a feeling it was. I was coming up the stairs when I heard the phone. Is anything wrong?'

'There is,' I said. 'Imogen Dale was murdered last night. Someone hit her over the head with a copper coal shovel. And the miniatures have been returned—I don't know how much you know about that—and I've told the police I came to see you to discuss a divorce. I said nothing about your knowing the Bodwells, or my having seen them, or Sir Oswald Smith-Ogilvie.'

'But do you want a divorce?' he said, sounding dismayed. 'You've never said anything about it before. Aren't you happy with things as they are?'

'Please listen,' I said. 'That's what I said I told the police. I don't know why I didn't tell them the truth and perhaps it was stupid, but I'd some idea of saving you trouble. So try not

142

to let me down now. Just remember we sat in the flat and decided to have a divorce and I never went to the pub or met the Bodwells. And if you can hide your connection with them you may manage not to get involved in this horrible affair down here, specially if you've an alibi for the later part of the evening. But I shouldn't invent one. The police are sure to catch you out. And I don't know where people like the Bodwells go when they want to disappear, but if I were you I'd tell them to go into hiding.'

There was silence on the line. I waited, giving him time to take in what I had said.

Then in a hushed, rather frightened tone, he said, 'I can't, Virginia.'

'Can't what?'

'Tell the Bodwells anything.'

'Why not?'

'They've gone.'

'Gone where?'

'I don't know. Soon after you left last night they packed their things and left. They said they were going to Scotland to look for a job there, but I don't know if that's where they really went. They aren't always absolutely truthful, you know. They may have gone anywhere.'

CHAPTER SEVEN

About two hours later the doorbell rang and I found Felix on the doorstep. It did not really surprise me. I had been half-expecting him all the afternoon, which I had spent restlessly cleaning out my kitchen cupboards, the kind of job that I normally put off to the last possible moment, but I could not have sat still.

All the same I asked him, not very warmly, 'What's brought you?'

'I want to know a lot more than you told me,' he said. His car was in the road and he had a small suitcase in his hand. Evidently he intended to stay. 'You're never very good on the telephone. I can always see you in my mind's eye counting the pence as they tick away. Anyway, I don't want you getting yourself in a mess with the police on my account. But you're dead wrong about the Bodwells, you know. They didn't steal the miniatures. How often have I got to tell you that?'

'Who did, then?'

I did not mention the fact that I was far less convinced that they had than I had been the evening before.

'I should have thought that was obvious.'

He had come in, shut the door and followed me into the sitting-room.

144

'Not to me,' I said. 'I haven't got your insight into the criminal mind.'

'There was nothing criminal about it. Well, relatively nothing.' He dropped on to the sofa and lit a cigarette. 'Don't tell me you can't sort out a simple thing like that.'

'You've always loved your little mysteries,' I said. I sat down too. 'I'm ready to wait for enlightenment.'

He inhaled deeply and let the smoke come dribbling out of his nostrils.

'Sarcasm, as usual,' he said. 'You'll never change, will you?'

'Will you? For instance, will you ever give up smoking?'

'Because it's lethal?' He smiled. 'Who cares if I live or die? I'm as unnecessary a person as you could meet. And who knows, I may be one of the lucky ones who smoke fifty a day and live to be eighty.'

'That's what everyone thinks about themselves.'

'I'll give it up when I can't afford it.'

'Don't tell me you're actually paying for all those cigarettes you smoke. Haven't you some cheap source of supply?'

'Well, occasionally I'm lucky and get them cheap from a chap I know, that's true, but it's irregular. And just think how few other vices I have. I drink far less than you do. But do I criticize you for it? I think one needs a vice or two to stay human.'

'Well, what about the miniatures?' I said. 'Who took them?'

'Nigel, of course.'

'But they're his. As you said yesterday yourself, he wouldn't have taken them.'

'That was before he returned them.' His vivid blue eyes, under their drooping lids, looked bright with secret knowledge. 'Just tell me when he discovered they'd been left to him.'

'I don't know,' I said. 'I haven't thought about it'

'As I remember what Imogen said to you that evening when she came here and I kept out of the room and just listened to the two of you talking, she told you that Mrs Arliss had left everything to her. Everything of importance, I think she said. And the miniatures aren't exactly unimportant, are they? So at that time she, and so probably Nigel too, believed they'd been left to her. But he's just the kind of person who'd think he had a right to them, and as it happens, I agree with him there. He's the only member of the family who's capable of appreciating them. Imogen would sell them without a second thought, but Nigel would treasure them. Tell me, did he arrive late at the funeral?'

There were times when Felix's intuitions gave me gooseflesh.

'He did, as a matter of fact.'

'There you are, then. He waited till the

others had started out to the funeral, collected the miniatures and hid them somewhere—it would have taken him only a few minutes—then went on after the rest of you to the church. He couldn't have known the Bodwells were going to help him by taking it into their heads to do a bolt because they were afraid of being suspected of theft. Then some time or other Huddleston told him the miniatures had been left to him and he realized that he'd stolen them from himself. A silly thing to have done, because if ever he wanted to display them he'd have to come out into the open about what he'd done. He'd the choice of admitting straight away that he'd taken them, which I imagine wouldn't have got him into any trouble, since they were legally his anyway, but would have made him look a bit of a fool, or returning them quietly when no one was about. Where was everyone yesterday evening?'

'They were all out until about half past ten. He'd the house to himself.' Memory was beginning to stir in my mind. 'It was after we all got back to the house after the funeral that Patrick told Nigel the miniatures had been left to him and Meg said they weren't insured, because Mrs Arliss had stopped paying the premiums. But if you're right, Felix, they can't have any connection with Imogen's murder, whereas if the Bodwells took them . . .' I paused, thinking it out.

'Can't you get that idea out of your head?' he said. 'If they had, they'd have told me.'

'Why?'

'We're very good friends. They wouldn't have kept a thing like that to themselves.'

'I haven't your faith in them. But your theory about Nigel is wonderfully neat and convenient. It gets everybody off the hook. But suppose he was late at the funeral only because he couldn't find his black tie or something and it actually was the Bodwells who took the miniatures . . .' I paused again. 'You said they left you yesterday immediately after I did and said they were going to Scotland, but suppose they'd taken me seriously and decided it would be best to return the miniatures before going off after a new job, they could just about have got to Allingford before Imogen and Patrick got back to the house, and just finished hanging up the miniatures when they heard the others come in. At first I thought they'd have bolted into the garden and so couldn't have had anything to do with the murder, but if in fact they were on their way back to the front door and so had to hide in one of the other rooms till after Patrick had gone, Imogen might have found them and perhaps threatened to call the police and Jim just might have lost his head and . . . No, that won't do. Why should she bother with the police if they'd brought the miniatures back? She was too generally lazy to be vindictive. Your idea about Nigel may be right.'

'Of course it is. It's nice and simple, isn't it? Nearly all good ideas are simple. You've got to get it out of your head that the murder and the theft and the Bodwells' leaving are somehow connected, simply because all three happened so close together. That was just chance. They were three quite separate events. Think of all the other separate events that were happening all over the world at the same time, the births and deaths and crimes and revolutions and floods and fires. You don't want to blame them all on the Bodwells, do you? Now what about going out to dinner this evening? I seem to remember the Rose and Crown isn't at all bad.'

The Rose and Crown was an old pub in the market place of Allingford. It had a Georgian frontage, with curved bay windows, but inside had the low ceilings and dark beams of a much earlier period. In recent times still more beams had been added, wherever there was room for them, to squeeze the last drop of the picturesque out of the place. In the immense fireplace in the bar, electrically operated logs flickered rhythmically and there were plentiful copper warming-pans and horse-brasses on the walls. The dining-room was dimly lit by candles on the tables and strip-lights concealed among the beams. I prefer to be able to see what I am eating, but I knew the food was excellent, if expensive.

I was not sure if Felix meant to pay for the meal, or whether at a certain stage he would start groping for my handbag, transferring several notes into his pocket, so that when the bill was presented he could appear to pay, having certainly given the waiter the impression that he was host. So I made sure before we went out that I had enough money with me to cover the cost, in case it should be needed, changed into a long dress, not because there was any need for formality at the Rose and Crown, but because I wanted to feel as different as possible from how I had felt all day, and realized while I was doing it that I was glad to be going out to dinner, even with Felix. I had done no shopping that day and if we had eaten at home it would have meant an omelet or opening some tins.

I let Felix order and as I watched him at it thought that his air of distinction, suitable to his age, was developing very nicely. I could not help wondering how he had come by it. On whom was he modelling himself? On his memories of his father? To the best of my knowledge, he had detested his father, but that did not mean that he had not deeply admired him. Not that I had any reliable information about him, but of all the different versions that Felix had given me of his childhood, the one that I most nearly believed was that his father had been in the army, marrying only after he had retired a woman much younger than himself, who in due course had left him, leaving Felix on his hands. His father had then taken up openly with another woman, and life in the Norfolk village where he had settled not being as permissive as it no doubt would be in these days, the family had been ostracized. Felix had grown up with the sense of being an outcast, starting early to find his only happiness in daydreams. To make matters worse, his father had been a violent man whose fits of almost maudlin affection for his son could change in a moment into mystifying rages. But he had seen to it that Felix had had a good education, though he had hated his school almost as much as his home. Authority of any kind was intolerable to him.

This story, I felt, was basically true, even if his father, who he had told me had been a colonel, had perhaps been only a sergeant and the public school to which he claimed he had been sent had been only the local grammar school. And such suspicions as those might be wrong. Felix was sometimes capable of telling the literal truth, even though he did it rather less convincingly than he told his lies.

He ordered smoked salmon, a dish of veal cooked with mushrooms and cream and a carafe of red wine.

As the waiter went away, I said, 'I wish I could understand something, Felix. Why did you really come to see me the other evening?

Wasn't it because you wanted to see the Bodwells?'

'You've got the Bodwells on the brain,' he said. 'Why should it have had anything to do with them? I told you I was in the neighbourhood and thought I'd like to see you.'

'I thought they might have let you know Mrs Arliss was dying,' I said, 'and you thought you might wheedle something out of her before she went.'

'Do you know, you sometimes terrify me,' Felix said. 'What a thing to imagine! I was quite fond of the old girl—you know that.'

'And she'd a bit of a soft spot for you, even though she disapproved of you. If you'd talked to her nicely, she might easily have given you some parting present to remember her by, even something quite valuable.'

'What d'you take me for—a vulture?' He drank some of his wine. 'Though, as a matter of fact, I believe the vulture is grossly maligned, chiefly because the poor beast's so ugly. It performs a most useful sanitary service and helps maintain the balance of nature. Have you noticed, by the way, what a sacred thing the balance of nature has become recently? I can't think why. Nature's been overbalancing in one direction or another ever since time began and the way man's helping it along these days, which is supposed to be so dreadful, is only a normal part of the process.'

I did not want to be side-tracked. 'You aren't ugly, like a vulture,' I said, 'and I can't see anything sanitary about relieving an old woman of some of her valuables, and if she didn't give you anything, you could easily have slipped some oddments into your pockets as you left. There'd have been no risk of getting into trouble, even if it was noticed. Your pals, the Bodwells, wouldn't have reported it, and Imogen and Nigel wouldn't have wanted to upset me. That is why you came, isn't it? Only you got here too late.'

'Have it your own way.' From him that was virtually an admission. 'I know there's no chance of getting you to change your mind about me once you've made it up. But my reasons for coming here today were just what I told you. I'm grateful to you for having tried to hide my connection with the Bodwells, but it really wasn't necessary and what I'd advise you to do now is to tell the police the truth.'

'I don't see how I can. I've rather committed myself, haven't I?'

'Not very seriously. People are always sympathetic to a woman who tries to protect her husband. And the fact is, I don't feel much in need of protection. I've no distrust of the Bodwells. I'm sure they were going straight all the time they were here and I'm sure they were nowhere near here last night, but on their way to Scotland, just as they told me. My theory about the murder is that it's connected with that woman's past—a jealous lover who didn't like being replaced by Huddleston, or something like that. Of course you know he and she have been lovers for some time, don't you?'

'I've supposed so during the last day or two,' I said, 'but how did you know?'

'I happened to see them once in a restaurant. It rather leapt to the eye.'

'He says that yesterday evening they decided to get married.'

'Does he now? *After* he discovered she hadn't got any money? Isn't that interesting?'

'You mean suspicious?'

'I don't, I mean exactly what I said. But I believe I've always found the behaviour of human beings more interesting than you ever have. It's something in me that's always been frustrated. If I'd had any outlet for it, it would have made all the difference in the world to me. I believe I ought to have been an artist of some kind, a writer or an actor perhaps, and if I hadn't had to scrounge for a living when I was young—'

'Felix,' I interrupted, 'I've heard that so often before and I think it may even be somewhere near the truth, except that even a writer or an actor has to put in a certain amount of concentrated hard work occasionally, but why are you trying to put it into my head that Patrick's a murderer?'

'But that's exactly what I'm not doing.'

154

'It isn't. You've gone at it deviously, but it's what you want me to think.'

'What I was actually trying to say about him is that whereas he can hardly have wanted to murder the woman he'd just got engaged to, obviously for love, not her money, since she hadn't any, a person who might have wanted to kill Imogen is that poor little secretary, Meg Randall. Not that I like the idea. She's so charming. She and I got on splendidly.'

'She's too small,' I said.

'Oh, I don't think so. Because she looks fragile, it doesn't mean she isn't strong. If she took Imogen by surprise, she could have done plenty of damage.'

'You aren't serious, are you?'

He did not answer.

Serious or not, I thought, if Felix could even dream up a theory like that, it was possible that the police might think on the same lines. Meg might find herself in trouble. I began to worry about her. She had not succeeded in disguising her feelings about Imogen from anyone and she had no alibi. She and Paul had gone upstairs together and said good night to one another in the passage before going to their rooms, but there was no one to say that she had not come downstairs again.

Only why should she have done that? If she had, it could hardly have been because she expected to find Imogen there. Then I remembered the light that had been on in the drawing-room when Nigel and I had discovered Imogen's body in the morning. Meg might have noticed the light showing under the door as she went upstairs, and come down again a few minutes later simply to switch it off. So she might have come on Imogen by chance, a happy and expansive Imogen, perhaps even a triumphant and cruel Imogen, who had taken pleasure in telling Meg of her engagement to Patrick, baiting the poor girl a little till she lost her head. Someone or other had lost their head, so why not Meg? There was something unpleasantly plausible about it.

Felix and I were eating in silence, like an old married couple who saw too much of each other to trouble with keeping up a conversation, when suddenly Felix said, 'There's Huddleston.'

Patrick had just come into the room and had seen us. He came towards us.

'Are you alone?' Felix asked. 'Come and join us.'

'May I?' Patrick drew out a chair at our table. 'When did you arrive? I knew you'd been here, but I thought you'd gone back to London.'

'Virginia telephoned me about Imogen, so I came back,' Felix said. 'I thought I might be useful.'

'I see.' Patrick sounded exhausted and distraught. When the waiter came to him he looked irritated at having to make up his mind about what he wanted to eat, then hardly glancing at the menu, ordered fillet steak. 'I don't know why I came out, except that I couldn't stand it at home. I was here yesterday with Imogen. Stupid to have come back tonight. I don't seem to be thinking clearly . . . Oh, thanks,' he added as Felix filled his glass with some of our wine. 'Tell me, Freer—I don't want to make an issue of it, I'm not in the mood for it—but am I right that you were Sir Oswald Smith-Ogilvie?'

'Since you put it like that,' Felix said, 'yes, I was. But how did you guess?'

Patrick put his elbows on the table and leant his head on his hands.

'It's just something that's been haunting me since it happened,' he said. 'It was when the Bodwells and the miniatures vanished at the same time and we were still taking it for granted the Bodwells had taken them, I said something about their having come with an excellent reference from a Sir Oswald Something—I couldn't remember his actual name—and Virginia came out with it straight off, though she'd far less reason to remember it than I had. Then she went red and looked furious with herself for having said anything. I thought at the time it was a bit strange, but I didn't pay it much attention, but when she said this morning that she went up to London to see you yesterday, I suddenly thought it could have been because she knew you'd written that

157

reference and were involved with the Bodwells. Because, after all, we all know what you're like and the sort of life you led her.' He drank some of his wine. 'No offence.'

Felix ate a mouthful of his veal before he answered. He looked as if he were deliberating just how much offence it would be reasonable to take. In the end he seemed to decide that it was not the time to take any.

'I want you to understand,' he said earnestly, 'that I only did what I could to help the Bodwells because I had the utmost faith in them. I knew they were sincere in wanting to start a new life, but I know more than you do, perhaps, about the difficulty of doing that once you've been in prison. I've done a fair amount of voluntary work among people in their sort of situation and I know there are times when one's justified in backing one's judgement and taking some degree of risk on their behalf. Of course I'd never have allowed them to go to Mrs Arliss if I hadn't been a hundred per cent sure I could trust them.'

The only voluntary work that Felix had ever done among the criminal classes, so far as I was aware, had consisted of drinking with them in pubs and I thought that Patrick probably knew this. He made an impatient gesture.

'None of that matters now,' he said. 'As a matter of fact, I think the Bodwells were quite good to Mrs Arliss. I know she thought she was very lucky having them to look after her. And at the end, when she really wasn't in her right mind any more, they were very kind to her. But I'd like to know where they are now.'

'That's funny,' Felix said reflectively.

'That I want to know where they are? It's just that I'd like to know if they took the miniatures, then for some reason, perhaps connected with that visit of Virginia's to London, brought them back. Because, if they did, you see, it's just possible they saw something of what happened in the drawing-room.'

'No, that isn't what I meant,' Felix said. 'I meant it's funny you should say how Mrs Arliss wasn't in her right mind at the end when the Bodwells told me she was absolutely normal. They said she was slightly paralysed down one side and her speech was a bit slurred, but that her mind was totally unaffected by the first stroke she'd had. They told me so quite positively.'

Patrick raised his head from his hands and gave Felix a long, thoughtful look which Felix returned as thoughtfully.

'I wonder why,' Patrick said.

'Why they told me that? Well, they knew I was interested in the old woman and wanted to know how she was.'

Also, no doubt, he had wanted to know how to handle her if he came to see her.

'No, no, why they were so sure she was

normal,' Patrick said. 'Because she did a very peculiar thing in the last week of her life, which suggests to me she was actually pretty confused. You see, she got me to the house and told me to destroy the last will she'd made, because, she said, she wanted to do the right thing by Imogen. In that last will, which I did destroy in accordance with her instructions, she'd left Imogen the miniatures and Nigel everything else, so it looked as if doing the right thing by Imogen meant leaving the money to her and the miniatures to Nigel. I didn't see anything strange about that at the time, because of course I didn't know there wasn't any money. But Mrs Arliss herself knew there wasn't and that what destroying that latest will meant was that she was totally disinheriting Imogen. So don't you think that Mrs Arliss had in fact forgotten that she hadn't any money? She wasn't so very normal after all, even if she appeared to be. She really didn't know what she was doing.'

This was just what Meg, Felix and I had discussed on the day after Mrs Arliss's death, but neither he nor I mentioned it.

The waiter put Patrick's fillet steak down in front of him and he began to eat. There was a curious obsessed look on his face, as if what he had been saying was immensely important to him.

'But what difference does any of this make now?' I asked. 'There can't be any connection between it and the murder, can there, and isn't that the only thing that matters?'

He gave such a start that I felt that bringing him back to the murder had been a dreadful act of cruelty. He put down his knife and fork as if he had discovered that he would not be able to eat another mouthful.

'I'm sorry, I'm not in a very rational state myself today,' he said. 'All kinds of things keep churning round in my mind. I suppose I'm thinking about that will I destroyed because of what the thought of all the money she was going to inherit meant to Imogen. D'you know, it was the reason she and I didn't get married long ago? She'd convinced herself I only wanted to marry her for her money and that if there wasn't any I'd want to break things off. I believe she was really deeply troubled about it and went on taking it for granted until last night when I managed at last to get her to believe the money didn't matter in the least and it was just herself I wanted. It was the first time she'd ever taken me seriously. I don't know how it would have worked out. We're both of us fairly difficult people. But you don't know how badly I wanted it.'

'I know I oughtn't to ask this,' I said, 'but did Meg ever mean anything to you?'

'Little Meg?' He gave a strained smile. 'You probably think I've treated her badly and perhaps I have. If so, it was mainly because I

161

didn't realize how emotional she was and how—well, how immature. But I don't think anything she feels about me goes very deep, you know. My impression is that it's getting transferred quite easily to Paul, who'll suit her far better than I ever should. And he seems to be extremely attracted to her, which is convenient in the circumstances. Anyway, for God's sake, don't blame me, Virginia, if I blundered about the girl. I didn't mean to and I've just about had as much as I can take today.'

He started again on his steak, but when he was about half way through it, gave it up and sat back.

'I was a fool to come out,' he said. 'I ought to have stayed at home. Thank you for putting up with me.'

He beckoned to the waiter for his bill.

Taking no notice of this, Felix said, 'About the Bodwells and your idea that they might have seen what happened in that room, what d'you think they'd have done if they had?'

Patrick gave a distracted frown. 'Weren't they blackmailers? That's what I gathered from the police. Wouldn't they have tried to cash in on what they saw?'

'So if you could find the Bodwells, you could probably find out who the murderer was.'

'So you know where they are,' Patrick said, suddenly alert. He turned to me. 'He does, doesn't he, Virginia?'

162

'I'm afraid I haven't the least idea,' I said. 'Do you, Felix? This is a serious thing, you know, not something to play with.'

'I only know what I told you,' Felix answered. 'They said they were going to look for a job in Scotland.'

Patrick's sallow face coloured a little. He leant towards Felix.

'I think you do know where they are. I think you're covering up for them.'

Felix shook his head. 'No.'

'I think they told you what they saw.' Patrick's voice was suddenly rasping. 'I think that's what brought you down.'

'To try a bit of blackmail myself?' Felix looked interested and not in the least angry.

'Why not?' Patrick had started to tremble. He seemed all at once to be in the grip of a violent rage. 'If the Bodwells were scared of getting involved in anything as dangerous as murder, that doesn't say you were too. What's a little murder, after all, if there's profit to be made out of it?'

'But I'm much more of a coward than either of the Bodwells,' Felix said, 'and I've never blackmailed anybody. It isn't one of my lines. Is it, Virginia?'

'Not to my knowledge,' I said.

'And if she'll admit that, you may rely on it,' he said.

'I honestly think you're quite wrong, Patrick,' I said. 'If Felix knew who'd done the murder, he'd keep as completely out of his way as he possibly could.'

Patrick looked intently from Felix's face to mine, then his rage seemed to leave him as abruptly as it had come.

'I'm sorry,' he said. 'I told you I wasn't rational. Forget what I said, will you? You've been very patient with me. I think I'd better spend the rest of the evening getting drunk at home. Goodbye.'

Looking as if he might break down somehow in another moment, he got up and made a stumbling rush for the door.

'Damn him,' Felix said, 'he didn't pay for his steak.'

'It doesn't matter,' I said. 'I've got plenty of money with me.'

'That's all right, so have I,' he said. 'A fair amount, anyway. But fillet steak's damned expensive. I may have to borrow a little. But I've got my banker's card, so I can cash a cheque tomorrow and pay you back. You know, I really wanted to give you a good evening out for once. But the poor chap simply doesn't know what he's doing, does he?'

In the end he borrowed four pounds from me, which was more than the fillet steak cost, but less than I had expected, though I thought that tomorrow he would discover that he had left his banker's card at home and would have to borrow some more.

Just then I did not mind. I was feeling

grateful for his company and mellowed by food and drink. As we went out to the car he put an arm round me and I leant comfortably against him. If only we could have arranged to see little enough of each other, I thought, we might have worked out some kind of happy marriage.

On the drive back to Ellsworthy Street he remarked, 'However, there's one thing I can tell you about Huddleston and that is that he's dead scared of the Bodwells.'

'How d'you make that out?' I asked.

'He kept trying to find out how much I knew about them, didn't he? He tried more than once and in different ways.'

'That needn't mean he's afraid of them, it could simply be that he thinks they may know something the police ought to know.'

'I think he's afraid.'

'But why?'

'Well, suppose he and Imogen didn't decide to get married last night. We've only his word for it that they did. Suppose he asked her to marry him, very pleased with his magnanimity because after all she hadn't the money they'd been waiting for, and she turned him down flat. Can't you see him going into a blind rage, just as he suddenly did this evening, only worse, and bashing her skull in out of sheer injured vanity?'

'And the Bodwells saw it and he's wondering when they're going to start making him pay for it? No, as a matter of fact, I can't see that happening. Patrick may be vain, but I'm sure he'd never risk his whole future for a reason like that.'

Felix sighed. 'I expect you're right. You know him much better than I do. But I rather wish I could get in touch with the Bodwells. I've started to wonder if they did come here yesterday evening before starting for Scotland. After all . . .' He paused.

He paused for so long that at last I said, 'Well?'

'Just a thought I had,' he said. 'Nothing important.'

From his tone I knew that he did not mean to say anything more about his thoughts, important or not. If I pressed him, I should only meet with evasions, so I said no more myself and we finished the drive in silence.

In the house we poured out final drinks for ourselves, then I switched on the radio, because it was time for the news and I always found that a dose of economic disaster, strikes, violent demonstrations, military coups and hijacking helped to send me sleepily to bed. I was already very sleepy. I sipped my drink and closed my eyes.

Then all of a sudden I was wide awake.

The impersonal voice of the announcer was saying, 'The bodies of the man and woman found shot dead in a car early this morning near the village of Deepstead, ten miles from

Allingford, have been identified as those of James and Rita Bodwell, for whom the police have been searching in the hope that they could help them with their enquiries into the murder of Imogen Dale.'

CHAPTER EIGHT

Felix grabbed the radio and looked as if he were going to try to shake more information out of it. Then as the cool voice went on to describe a minor massacre in one of the confusing new nations in Africa, he switched it off, but he stayed where he was, frowning at the small transistor, his face unusually pale. I saw bewilderment and hesitation on it. He rubbed a hand along his jaw, biting on his lower lip.

After a moment he said, 'Virginia, why don't you come back to London with me tonight?'

'Why should I do that?' I asked.

'If I leave you here, you'll get mixed up in this business,' he said, 'and they're dangerous people. I'd be happier if I knew you were safely out of it.'

'Who's dangerous?'

'One of them—Nigel, Paul, Huddleston. Even Meg. She could have held a gun.'

'Where did she get it?'

'How should I know? But it has to be one of them.'

'Aren't you jumping to conclusions?' I said. 'The Bodwells had their criminal past. Isn't it probable that someone belonging to it followed them down here and shot them? You

168

said yourself I shouldn't assume that all the things that have been happening are connected.'

He shook his head. 'It's a bit too much of a coincidence, the thing having happened so close to Allingford. They must have come down here last night and seen Imogen's murder, then tried to squeeze something out of the murderer and got shot for it.'

'Why shot? Or rather, since he had a gun, why didn't he use it on Imogen too, instead of a clumsy thing like a copper shovel.'

He gave an irritated click of his tongue.

'I can't tell you everything. Meanwhile, I don't like to think of you mixing with that lot. They're trouble.'

'But I'm not dangerous to anybody. I don't know anything.'

He came close to me, put his hands on my shoulders and shook me.

'Virginia, would you just for once do something I ask you? Come back to London with me.'

I disengaged myself. 'I'm sorry, Felix, but I think it would be a stupid thing to do. It would make the police start thinking I've something to hide. But stay here yourself if you're feeling so protective.'

'All right, if that's how you feel.'

'What brought them here, d'you think?' I asked. 'Why didn't they go straight to Scotland, if they ever meant to go there at all?'

He seemed not to hear the question. I repeated it.

His voice suddenly went high with exasperation. 'How the hell should I know? They said they were going.'

'Weren't they bringing the miniatures back?'

'No, no, no! They never took them.'

'How d'you know? They didn't tell you everything about themselves, did they? Or did they? Are you so sure about the miniatures because you know the real reason why they came?'

I saw his hands clenching and unclenching, as if he were having to make a great effort to keep his temper.

'Listen,' he said in a tone of desperate patience, 'it may not have occurred to you, but they were friends of mine. Hearing about their deaths like that has been a pretty bad shock and having you going on and on firing questions at me isn't exactly helping. The next thing you'll be suggesting, if I know you, is that I had something to do with it. Whatever happens, I'm always to blame, I know that. I don't expect anything else from you. But I should have thought, just this once, you might have been a little considerate.'

'But I haven't blamed you for anything,' I said. 'And I'm sure you had nothing to do with their deaths. Violence, like blackmail, isn't one of your lines. It just struck me you might know the reason why they came.'

He shook his head. 'I don't know any more about it than you do. You needn't look so sceptical. Oh God, why did I ever come here the other night? D'you know, I thought you might help me. The older I get, the more I want to change my way of living. The more I want to be the sort of person you'd like me to be. And I came here, hoping for a—well, you could call it a refuge, while I put in a little practice at being a sober, responsible citizen. And all you could think of was that I'd come to steal some knick-knacks from a dying woman.'

'My poor old skeleton in search of a cupboard to hide in,' I suggested. 'Oh, Felix, if I hadn't heard it all so often before . . . But stay here as long as you like. I'm sure that'll be wiser than dashing off to London. The police are certain to want to question you sooner or later. If I were you, I'd go to them without waiting for them to come looking for you.'

He gave me a gloomy sigh. 'You may be right. I'll think about it. Perhaps I'll go to them in the morning.'

There was no need for him to do that, however, because they came to us. We were at breakfast when they came, not Superintendent Chance, but the curly-haired sergeant and a detective-constable.

I had had another restless night. I had kept thinking of the appeal that Felix had made to me the evening before and which I had automatically refused, having listened to him too often in the past saying the very same things. But supposing that just for once he had meant what he said, had my refusal to help him been anything but cold-hearted and self-righteous?

I had thought that I was cured of ever worrying about this problem again. I had made up my mind long ago never to believe in any of his promises of reformation and at the same time I had recognized that I should never be able to accept the only kind of life of which he seemed to be capable. Attempting to do it in the old days had made me profoundly unhappy.

Yet there was something about him that always upset my judgement and made me think that perhaps I ought to make one more try. It was a strange fact that even after all these years he still seemed to feel some genuine affection for me and affection is not in such excess supply that what there is should be thoughtlessly thrown away.

In the night hours this thought had loomed particularly large. I knew that it would be easier to hold on to common sense in the daytime, but lying alone and sleepless in the darkness, the yearning to have someone love me again, even if he was not exactly perfect, had grown so intense that it had scared me. At one moment I felt certain that to give in to it would be the limit of absurdity, then at the next a creeping doubt set in that to resist it was the true stupidity. The result was that when Felix brought me a cup of tea in bed I had treated him with irritable ingratitude, as if he were to blame for my night of conflict, and this had hurt his feelings so much that when we met at breakfast we were both silent and sullen. The arrival of the police was a distraction.

We took them into the sitting-room. As we all sat down the innocent-looking young sergeant asked if we had heard the news about the Bodwells. I said that we had heard it on the radio the evening before.

'Ah yes, the radio,' he said, making it sound as if it were an astonishing new invention. He looked at Felix. 'You knew them, I believe, sir.'

'Yes,' Felix answered. 'I suppose Mr Huddleston told you that.'

'That's right, sir. He said you gave them a reference when they applied for work with Mrs Arliss.'

'Didn't he say I forged a reference for them?'

'I was coming to that.' The sergeant smiled cheerfully, as if forging references was a clever trick that he could not help admiring. 'You knew them pretty well, then?'

'Fairly well,' Felix said.

'You knew about their records?'

'Oh yes.'

'When did you see them last?'

'The day before yesterday, in the evening. I think it was soon after nine o'clock. They came to me when they left here and I think they were intending to stay with me for a day or two, till they made up their minds what to do next, but my wife came up to see me that evening and when she found them with me, threatened to tell the police where they were unless they returned the miniatures she was sure they'd stolen. She was quite wrong about that, as it happens, but they took fright and decided to leave for Scotland to look for new jobs there.'

The sergeant turned to me. 'Yes, as a matter of fact, Mrs Freer, you were wrong about that. Mr Tustin has admitted he removed the miniatures himself, then later, finding what disturbance it caused, decided to return them. He was questioned last night, when it became evident that the Bodwells had been in the vicinity and it seemed just possible that it was they who'd returned the miniatures. But whatever brought them can't have had anything to do with that.'

Felix gave me a glance of the I-told-you-so variety.

'I was sure Tustin had taken them,' he said.

'We'd like to know, though, can you tell us anything about what really brought the Bodwells?' the sergeant went on.

Felix took a moment to think over his answer, then shook his head.

'But are you sure they came here at all?' he asked. 'Weren't they found some distance from Allingford? That's what it said on the radio.'

'Yes, the car in which they were found had been driven off the main road a hundred yards up a farm lane near the village of Deepstead,' the sergeant answered. 'That's about ten miles from here. And it isn't actually certain they ever came here, though it looks probable, you must admit.'

'I should have thought myself this was the last place they'd come to,' Felix said.

'Then you don't know of any reason why they might've come?'

'No, all I know is, they said they were going to Scotland.'

'Did you see them leave?'

'I saw them put their things in their car and drive off, if that's what you mean.'

'They hadn't by any chance any passenger?'

'No.'

'Because someone drove them to Deepstead, whether it was from here or from London. Bodwell was in the seat beside the driver's and Rita Bodwell was at the back. Neither did the driving. In fact, they were probably both dead before the drive began. If the murderer had wanted to make them drive to that quiet spot before killing them, he'd have sat with his gun jammed into the driver's neck and told him where to go. Unless, of course, he was someone they trusted.' He

175

turned to me again. 'What time did you last see them, Mrs Freer?'

'I suppose about half past eight,' I said. 'We sat and talked in a pub called the Waggoners, near the end of Little Carbery Street, then I left and got home about half past ten. I told Mr Chance when I got home, though I didn't tell him I'd seen the Bodwells.'

The sergeant plainly knew this. 'Yes. And you, Mr Freer? Would you mind telling me what you did after the Bodwells left you?'

Felix gave an abrupt laugh. 'So I'm the person you think they trusted, am I?'

'It's just a matter of routine, sir,' the sergeant said.

'Can you tell me, how did I get away after I killed them?' Felix asked.

'The murderer got away in one of two ways,' the sergeant answered patiently. 'Either he had a car parked up the lane in waiting and drove away in it—the heavy rain would have obliterated all tracks—or else he walked.'

'In which case he must have got pretty wet.'

'I should say so. Now what about where you were that evening?'

Felix appeared to meditate. In fact, I was sure that he had his answer ready and had no need to think about it, but he felt that it would be appropriate to seem a little uncertain.

'Let me see,' he said. 'The day before yesterday. Yes, I remember. My wife had gone home and the Bodwells had left and what with

176

one thing and another I was feeling restless, so I went back to the Waggoners and I met some friends of mine there, John and Myrtle Lewis, who live in Little Carbery Street, too, at number sixty-six. We stayed till closing-time, then I went home with them. I think I stayed until about one o'clock. John Lewis is a great talker and it was one of his evenings for explaining how the world should be set to rights. My own view, as I told him, is that nothing will set it to rights till the medical profession comes up with some pill that will basically change human nature. A gloomy view, you may think. However, that isn't what you want to know, is it? It's just my alibi. Well, Mr and Mrs Lewis will confirm it.'

'Thank you, sir.' The sergeant made a note of the Lewis's address, then he looked at me once more. 'There's nothing you'd like to add, Mrs Freer?'

'No,' I said.

'You're sure you can't think of any reason why the Bodwells might have wanted to return to Allingford?'

'I'm afraid not, unless they wanted to fetch something they'd left behind, or something quite simple like that.'

'And saw the murder of Miss Dale.'

'That's possible, isn't it?'

'Yes, but I've a feeling—oh well, that's all it is, a hunch, nothing to build on—that the reason that brought them back is central to our whole enquiry. If you can think of anything—anything at all—that might shed light on it, we'd be very grateful if you'd get in touch with us.'

He thanked us then for our helpfulness and he and the constable left.

When they had gone I went to the kitchen, stacked the breakfast dishes in the dishwasher, then went upstairs and made the beds. Coming downstairs again, I put on my coat, then looked into the sitting-room. Felix was lying on the sofa in one of his dreamy states, staring up at the ceiling, a cigarette dangling between his fingers. But hearing me at the door, he looked round and seeing my coat, asked me where I was going.

'I'm going to talk to Nigel,' I said. 'There's something I want to ask him. D'you want to come with me?'

'I don't think so,' he said. 'I didn't sleep well. I'm feeling rather tired.'

'Don't you want to phone your friends, the Lewises?'

'Why should I do that?'

'To tell them what to say to the police about the evening you're supposed to have spent with them.'

'You mean you don't believe me about what I did?'

'As you know, the trouble is, I never know when to believe you and when not.'

He sat up abruptly. 'Are you telling me you

178

think I'm the trusted person that bloody sergeant was talking about who drove the Bodwells to Deepstead? My God, what will you think of next? And why Deepstead, of all places? I never even knew it existed till I heard about it on the radio last night.'

'Whoever left them there may have wanted it to look as if they must have come from Allingford, so that someone here would be suspected.'

He looked incredulous. 'That's altogether too complicated for me. I'm a simple soul, you know. I don't understand things like that. But you needn't worry, what I told the sergeant about the Lewises is the exact truth. I shouldn't be such a fool as to invent a story like that.'

I thought that was probably true and telling him that I was not sure when I should be back, I went out, leaving him to his chain-smoking and dreaming.

As I turned into the drive up to the Arliss house I found a lorry blocking the way and men at work, dismembering the fallen elm. Backing my car out of the gate and leaving it in the road, so that it would not be in the way of the lorry if it should be driven away soon, I walked towards the house across the lawn.

The morning was mild and faintly misty and the grass felt moistly spongy under my feet. Looking up at the house, I had a curious fancy that there had been some change in its aspect since I had seen it last. But at most this was an illusion caused by the mist, which made it seem to have retreated to a greater distance than usual. All the same, it seemed to me to have developed a new, impenetrable expression on its not very handsome face, a blankness put on to conceal heaven knew what secrets. The house, after all, knew everything that had happened here two nights ago. Houses always know everything.

Passing the tree and the great hole where its roots had been torn up, I found myself suddenly face to face with Nigel. He was standing watching the work with his hands locked behind him and the look on his face of someone who felt that the work would not be properly done unless he kept an eye on it.

'Ah, Virginia,' he said when he saw me, 'you've heard this extraordinary news about the Bodwells, of course. Shocking and dreadful. And for certain connected in some way with Imogen's death, though I fail to see how. Have you any theories about it?'

'Only that they must have seen the murder and tried to cash in on it,' I said. 'They were given to blackmail. But there's a question that Felix and I were talking over this morning. I wonder if you've any ideas about it. Imogen was killed with that copper shovel. The Bodwells were shot. But if the murderer had a gun, why didn't he shoot Imogen?'

'A good question,' Nigel said. 'I hadn't

considered it. As you say, why didn't he? But at least I can tell you where the gun came from. I was able myself to tell the police that. My uncle had a revolver that dated from the first world war and it was always kept in the bottom drawer of the bureau in the morning-room. I can remember him taking it out and showing it to me when I was a child, though he would never talk about anything to do with the war. But he kept the gun as a trophy and when he died Aunt Evelyn kept it in memory of him. It means, of course, that the murderer of the Bodwells must be someone from this house, who knew where the gun was kept, not some criminal associate of theirs from London. As a matter of fact—' he dropped his voice confidentially— 'it's one of the reasons why I came out this morning. I was driven out by the conviction that one of the people in it is a murderer. Oh, not exactly in it, because Patrick must be included as a suspect. And from your point of view, I can see I may be one.' He gave a nervous little laugh. 'I suppose you've heard about my appalling indiscretion with the miniatures.'

'That you stole them from yourself?' I said. 'That's true, is it?'

'Absolutely true, I'm afraid. And it's so unlike me, isn't it? I mean, to yield to an impulse like that. An insane impulse. Because that's what it was when I took them, pure insanity. After all, I'm not normally a creature of impulse, am I? Would you say I was?'

There were few people I could think of who were less impulsive than Nigel.

'Rather decidedly not,' I replied. 'But I suppose we all have our weak moments.'

'I did it in anger,' he went on. 'I thought they'd been left to Imogen and that she was utterly incapable of appreciating them. They're very beautiful, you know, apart from their value. I shan't think of selling them. Then after the funeral I discovered they'd been left to me. I suppose the sensible thing at that point would have been to admit I'd taken them. After all, I'd done nothing illegal. But my courage failed me and that evening, when everyone else was out of the house, I thought how easy it would be to return them to their proper places. And I thought I was going to get away with it. But when I heard of the death of the Bodwells, I felt I had to tell the police the truth. There was the idea everyone had, you see, that the Bodwells had stolen them and for some mysterious reason they'd come back and returned them and that that had something to do with their getting murdered. So it seemed to me it was my duty to confess I was the culprit. Very humiliating. I felt the worst kind of fool. But I'm glad now it's done and that I haven't got it on my conscience any longer.'

'The police asked me if I'd any idea what could have brought the Bodwells back,' I said.

182

'I told them I hadn't.'

'So did I. So did Patrick. So did Paul. So did Meg. I fancy one of us is lying, but I don't know which.'

'The gun does seem to tie it down to one of you.'

He gave a tight little smile. 'Not forgetting that we should perhaps include you, my dear Virginia. You knew your way about the house well enough to have known where the gun was. Not to mention Felix. Patrick told me this morning that he's down here again.'

'Yes, he came down as soon as he heard of Imogen's murder.'

'Has he some information about it, then?'

'No, but he likes to be where the action is. He's very inquisitive. Now I think I'll go in and talk to Meg.'

'Yes, do that. Poor child, she's very young to be mixed up in a terrible business like this. Not that I think the young are as sensitive to horror as we older ones. Remembering my own war experiences, it seems to me I was amazingly callous and cold-blooded in those days.'

He gave me a little nod of farewell and strolled away down the lawn.

I found Meg in the kitchen, listlessly washing a lettuce. She was even paler than usual and was stooping over the sink as wearily as if she had suddenly grown old. She turned when she heard me come in and gave me a vague smile.

183

'Cooking isn't really my job,' she said. 'I'm a secretary. But somebody has to do it. Mrs Jones, who helped Mrs Bodwell with the cleaning, rang up to say she wasn't going to go on coming to a house where there'd been a murder. And the police want us all to stay here and we've got to be fed. Paul offered to take me out to lunch, but I didn't feel much like it. I feel like hiding. Do you ever feel like that? Paul says the press are sure to descend on us soon and if they do I think I'll go mad.'

'If they do come, I'd leave Nigel to cope with them,' I said. 'He'll do it very adequately. There's no reason why they should bother you. Can I help you with getting lunch?'

'Oh, I'm not doing anything much and there's no hurry.' She began tearing the lettuce into small pieces, looking as if she had a grudge against it. 'The worst of it is, I'm horribly frightened. Aren't you?'

'In a way, I suppose. Frightened by the thought of what may come out. Is that what you mean?'

'I think I mean frightened at finding out what life can be like. Everything's suddenly different from what I thought it was and it's never going to be the same again. I expect that sounds awfully childish to you.'

'It's something that most of us go through some time or other,' I said. It had happened to me when I had begun to find Felix out. 'But if we're lucky, it's a bit more gradual than it's

184

been for you. Did the police question you last night?'

'Yes, but only that sergeant. He was quite nice. He didn't seem to think I was a murderer. But they wouldn't show it, I suppose, even if they thought so. Mr Chance talked for ages to Mr Tustin. He told him about the revolver in the drawer of the bureau. Do you know about that?'

'He's just been telling me about it himself,' I said. 'I met him in the garden. But are they sure that's the gun that was used? Have they found it?'

'I don't think so. After all, the murderer wouldn't just leave it lying around, would he? He'd throw it away somewhere. But the one Mrs Arliss had hidden away is missing, so it's almost sure to be the one that was used.'

She had abandoned the lettuce and sat down at the kitchen table. Her white face looked very tired.

'Who thought of looking for it?' I asked. 'Who found out it was missing?'

'Mr Tustin,' she answered. 'When the police came here and told us about the Bodwells he simply walked straight to the bureau and opened the bottom drawer and said, "Ah, that's interesting," and then told the police all about it.'

'So from the start he was sure the Bodwells had been killed by someone from this house, or someone who knew his way about it.'

She gave me a woeful nod.

'And if it had been him, he wouldn't have drawn attention to the revolver being missing, would he?' she said.

And that left Patrick and Paul, two people to whom she was strongly attracted, though which of them meant the more to her at the moment I should not have liked to guess. I thought that she herself might not know this for sure, a state of affairs that would increase the mood of anxiety and confusion that she was in.

To comfort her, I said, 'Perhaps Nigel was just being over-subtle. Perhaps he's our murderer after all.'

She looked at me searchingly. It was a possibility that she liked, but she said, 'You don't really mean that.'

'I'm not sure,' I said. 'I think he'd make a pretty good murderer. According to him, he was awfully ferocious during the war. He's used to having blood on his hands. The trouble is, I can't think of any reason why he should have murdered Imogen. He doesn't seem to have any motive.'

'Or for killing the Bodwells either.'

'The Bodwells were killed because they saw Imogen's murder, that's simple,' I said. 'Meg, tell me something. You knew the Bodwells better than any of us. Can you think of anything they might have known about somebody here which they might have used for blackmail? Because I'm sure that's why they came down that evening. They wanted to extort all they could before setting off to look for a job in Scotland.'

I was not expecting any enlightening answer to my question. I was sure she knew nothing. But I was not expecting the reaction that I got either. She gave me one swift look of horror, then burst violently into tears.

She cried noisily, like a child, curling her hands into fists and thrusting them into her eyes. Her small, slim body jerked convulsively. All the pent-up emotions of the last few days, going back perhaps as far as Mrs Arliss's death, streamed out of her in hiccuping sobs.

The door opened and Paul came in.

'What the hell have you been doing to her?' he shouted at me furiously, then he swept her up into his arms. After looking for a moment as if she would push him away, she hid her face on his shoulder and clung to him.

He looked at me over her head. I had never imagined that his young, good-natured face could look so malevolent.

'Is this your doing?' he demanded.

'It won't do her any harm,' I said. 'It's time she had a good cry.'

'But what set it off?'

'It doesn't matter.'

'Of course it matters. What have you been saying to her?'

'Why not ask her yourself? We were talking

187

and it just overflowed. I think it's quite natural.'

He gave me a worried frown, uncertain whether or not to believe me.

'Meg, darling,' he said hesitantly, 'what's this all about?'

She gave a louder wail and clung to him more tightly. He touched her hair gently, stroking it away from her face, then kissed her forehead. I thought it was time that I left them.

But before I reached the door, Paul said, 'You frightened her, didn't you? You said something that scared the living daylights out of her.'

'I don't know, perhaps I did,' I answered and left the kitchen.

I drove home and found Felix lying on the sofa, exactly where I had left him. He might not have moved all the time that I had been away, except for the fact that there were more cigarette stubs than before in the saucer beside him.

Looking up at me, he asked, 'Well, what did you get out of Nigel?'

'Some quite interesting things,' I said.

'I was right about the miniatures, wasn't I?' Felix said. 'Only you wouldn't believe it till you heard it from the police.'

'Nigel told me that the gun that was used to shoot the Bodwells was probably one that belonged to Mrs Arliss,' I said. 'She kept it in a drawer in a bureau and it's vanished.'

'Mrs Arliss kept a gun? How extraordinary people are, aren't they? Who'd ever have thought of such a thing?'

'I also saw Meg.' I took off my coat and tossed it on to a chair. 'I want a drink.'

'What do you want—whisky?'

'Please.'

He went out, muttering disapprovingly to himself, and returned after a moment with a drink for each of us.

'What was that you said about Meg?' he asked as he sat down again.

'Just that I'd seen her. But there's something funny about her, Felix. I simply asked her if she knew anything the Bodwells might have known about anyone in that household and she went into a fit of hysteria. She wept and wailed and shook all over. And Paul came in and accused me of having frightened her and the odd thing is, I think I had.'

Felix took a cautious sip of his drink, then put it down at arm's length from him, as if to make sure it lasted while I had two or three.

'So she does know something that she's keeping to herself,' he said. 'Or perhaps she's only just understood the meaning of it. And now the strain's too much for her. It's something to do with Huddleston, of course.'

'That's what I thought myself. I don't think she'd cover up for anyone else, even for Paul.

189

And anyway, the Bodwells hardly knew Paul.'

'No.' A deep thoughtfulness came over Felix. His eyelids drooped till his eyes were almost closed. Wrinkles appeared on his high forehead. Locking his hands together, he seemed for a moment to go into a mild sort of trance, or at least to forget that he was not alone. Some problem of his own was taking up the whole of his attention. But suddenly his eyes snapped open and his bright blue gaze fastened on my face. 'I'd hoped I shouldn't have to say anything about this,' he said, 'but I'd better admit I haven't been absolutely frank with you about the Bodwells.'

'You truly astonish me,' I said.

'No, don't talk like that, this is serious.' He passed a hand across his forehead in a gesture that erased the wrinkles from it and left him with his blandest face. 'You see, they were my friends. I trusted them. I stuck out my neck for them. I was absolutely convinced they'd made up their minds never to dabble in blackmail again. And they told me something about Huddleston and said what it would be worth to them if they felt like using it, but they were both laughing and there was something about the way they laughed which made me certain they weren't even thinking of using it, the whole thing was just a joke. And that's why I haven't said anything about it before. I thought it would only complicate things and not be fair to their memory. My friends are very

190

important to me, as you know, and I should hate to be disloyal to them.'

It was not entirely hypocrisy. A friend, whatever he was like, helped to reassure Felix that he was not as inadequate as at times, under the surface, he recognized that he was. But I was not in a mood to be much moved by this.

'What's this leading up to?' I asked.

'The thing the Bodwells told me about Huddleston,' he said.

'What was it?'

'Quite a small thing. It seems that after Mrs Arliss had her first stroke she summoned him and made him draw up a new will for her—'

I interrupted, 'She got him to destroy a will.'

'No, that's just the point,' Felix said. 'That's what the Bodwells knew. He drew up a will for her there and then and the Bodwells came in and witnessed her signature. And it's that will that he destroyed on the quiet, a will in which, I imagine, she left her money to Nigel and the miniatures to Imogen. She talked about wanting to do the right thing by Imogen, didn't she? And she knew the miniatures were the only valuable things she had left. But Huddleston didn't know that. He thought she had lots of money and that her poor old mind was wandering and that if he destroyed that last will the one before it would stand and all that nice money would go to Imogen, whom he hoped to marry. A regrettable blunder and highly unprofessional and it was that that put him in the power of the Bodwells. That's why he tried so hard yesterday evening to find out what I knew about them. And I'm afraid it's what brought them down here the other evening. In spite of the promises of reform they'd made to me, they wanted to squeeze what they could out of him before setting off for Scotland.'

'How did they know he was saying Mrs Arliss had asked him to destroy a will and not make a new one?' I asked.

'Rita overheard him saying that to Meg, even before Mrs Arliss died.'

'I see. Yes. Then you think they came down here to get some money from Patrick, somehow found out he'd gone to the Arliss house with Imogen, followed him there, saw him murder Imogen through the french window, thought they'd cash in on that in a much bigger way than they'd originally intended and ended up dead. Only why should Patrick murder the woman he was going to marry? That's something you still haven't told me.'

'I've suggested a possibility. Injured vanity when she turned him down.'

'I don't believe that.'

'Then why not Imogen's injured vanity? If he refused to marry her without any money and if she turned on him and threatened to get the Bodwells to expose what he'd done about

192

the will, mightn't he have lost his head and killed her?'

193

CHAPTER NINE

I turned his suggestion over in my mind for a little while. After a time I said, 'It's not impossible.'

'But you aren't impressed.'

'I don't know. I've lost the feeling I know anything at all about any of those people. A few days ago I'd have said that all the things that have happened were unthinkable.' I stood up. 'I'll get some lunch. Just sandwiches, I'm afraid.'

'That'll be fine.'

I went to the door, but paused there. 'Felix, it sounds melodramatic, but if there's anything in the things we've been saying, mightn't Meg be in danger?'

'I wouldn't say she isn't,' he answered.

'Of course, she doesn't really know anything, she's only guessing.'

'Unless the Bodwells mentioned to her some time that they'd witnessed a will. I don't know if they did or not.'

'Well, oughtn't we to go to the police?'

'To tell them what the Bodwells told me? Why should they believe me?'

'Why shouldn't they?'

'Because Huddleston will deny it and it'll be only my word against his. And he's a respected citizen.'

There was something in that. I went to the kitchen, opened a tin of ham and made some sandwiches and coffee. While I was doing it I wondered, as I often had before, what it felt like to be Felix. He was usually so confident that any outrageous thing which he felt like saying would of course be believed, yet at the same time, at the back of his mind, he seemed to find it only natural that he should not be trusted. And the closer he stuck to the truth, the more he appeared to expect to be doubted. Something in him was always deeply afraid of being found out. Sometimes I felt there was a pathos in this which made me want to protect him, though I knew that it would not really do any good. Trying to protect Felix from himself was just a wonderful way of wasting time.

Putting the sandwiches and coffee on a tray, I took them into the sitting-room.

After we had had our lunch I told him that I was going out shopping and set off for Whitefield's to buy something for us to eat in the evening. Although it was some distance to the market place I walked instead of driving, because I wanted some time to myself to turn some things over quietly in my mind. I was not in the mood for the kind of cooking that would need much attention, so I only bought chops, a cauliflower and some fruit, but buying food for the two of us, instead of just for myself, gave me a not unpleasant feeling of nostalgia. I almost enjoyed doing it. When I started the walk home I realized that I had done very little of the thinking that I had intended, but had only mooned stupidly about the attractions of buying two chops instead of one and a cauliflower that was not the smallest on the shelf and that this was dangerous when Felix himself was showing signs of a homing instinct.

I walked slowly, giving myself time to remember that life with Felix was unendurable, anyway for me. There must be women, I thought, whom he could make very happy. To be fair to him, it was his misfortune as much as mine that his affections had ever attached themselves to me.

When I opened my front door I heard voices in the sitting-room. The visitor was Nigel. When I joined him and Felix, after taking my shopping basket to the kitchen, he rose from his chair, said, 'Ah, Virginia,' as if it was mildly surprising to find me in my own home, and stood there, looking at me with a grave concern which immediately filled me with alarm.

'What's wrong?' I asked quickly.

'It's Meg,' he said. 'She would seem to have disappeared. I came here to see if by any chance she'd come to you. Felix tells me you haven't seen her.'

'Not since this morning,' I said. 'But what do you mean, disappeared?'

'Just that she seems to have left the house without telling anyone.'

'When?'

'We don't know. I was expecting her to get lunch and it occurred to me after a time that it was getting rather late, but I didn't like to make any comment, as it's really very good of her to be looking after us at all, so I waited for some time longer and then at about a quarter past two I thought there must be something wrong and went looking for her and found she was nowhere in the house. I searched it thoroughly and the garden too and there wasn't any sign of her.'

'Where was Paul all this time?' I asked. 'Wasn't he getting worried too?'

'I'm not sure, but I think the two of them had a quarrel,' Nigel said. 'I found him going through the books Aunt Evelyn left him, sorting out the ones he didn't want, and when I asked him if he'd seen Meg, he only grunted in a surly sort of way and said he didn't want any lunch anyhow.'

'They were anything but quarrelling when I saw them last,' I said, remembering the sobbing Meg held in Paul's loving arms. 'But if they did have a row of some sort, doesn't that explain what's happened to her? She simply walked out of the house to get away from him for the time being.'

'I'm sure that's all that's happened,' Felix said.

At once I felt sure that it was not what had happened, or at least that Felix did not think it had. I knew his tones of voice so well that I could easily tell that he did not believe what he had said. Besides, there was the nagging fear in my mind that Meg was in possession of what might be dangerous knowledge.

'Did she take anything with her?' I asked. 'A suitcase or anything?'

Nigel looked slightly embarrassed. 'I'm afraid I'm not very well acquainted with what a young girl would take with her if she suddenly saw fit to vanish. I did look into her bedroom and it's my impression that if she took anything it can't have been much. Her wardrobe was full of dresses, her drawers were full of—of stockings and such things. There were cosmetics and a hair-brush on her dressing-table. But when I induced Paul to help me search, we agreed that her handbag seemed to be missing. I know that looks as if she suddenly decided just to go out and have lunch by herself, because she needed to get away from Paul and me, not to mention the house, and yet I'm concerned. To tell the truth, I'm in a very edgy state of mind today and find myself tending to imagine the worst. However, you think that's stupid of me, I gather.'

'From your point of view, what would the worst be?' Felix asked.

'Why, that some harm had come to her.'

'Not that she'd simply decided to go to the police?' We had all sat down. Nigel had a hand

198

on each plump knee and kept looking from one to the other of us, as if he hoped to catch on one of our faces some expression that would reveal something of importance.

'The police!' he exclaimed. 'Good heavens, I never thought of that. Do you think she knew something then, or thought she did, about these ghastly events that she thought she ought to tell them? It was after they came to the house that she must have gone. Do you think they may have said something to her that started her thinking about something she knew but hadn't understood before? I suppose that's possible.'

'Have you had the police in the house again, then?' I asked, realizing only after I had said it that it made the police sound like some vermin that had invaded the premises.

Nigel went on massaging his knees. 'Oh yes,' he said, 'they wanted to look at all our shoes. For mud, you know, in case one of us had driven the bodies of the Bodwells out to that lane where they were found and then walked home, getting caught in the rain. A very long walk on a night like that. I shouldn't have cared to undertake it myself. I'm not sure what the police thought of us all, but they took away all the shoes we'd been wearing that evening. Mine happened to have been polished. I do that every morning, but I couldn't help feeling they thought there was something suspicious about my having done it. And Meg and Paul each had mud on a pair of shoes, but as you may remember, they went out shopping together after breakfast on the morning after the storm and just walking down the drive, dodging the puddles, would have been enough to make their shoes muddy.'

'I remember I got mine fairly muddy just walking up the drive and past the tree,' I said. 'But do you think Meg's disappearance has anything to do with that?'

'I wish I knew,' Nigel answered. 'But I understand you think I'm worrying unduly.'

'Not necessarily,' Felix said. 'But I'd wait for a bit and see if she turns up soon, then if she doesn't, get in touch with the police. If she went to them, I shouldn't think they'd keep her long. You may even find she's back at the house by the time you get there.'

'I hope so.' Nigel got to his feet. 'Yes, I hope so. But I'm a worrying type. After what's happened already I can't help thinking she may have got herself into some kind of trouble, dreadful trouble. There's someone ruthless amongst us, ruthless and dangerous. And she seems to me a very innocent sort of girl. Very trusting. Oh dear, I do hope you're right there's nothing to worry about.'

He made for the door. I saw him out of the house, then returned to the sitting-room. Felix had just stretched himself out again at full length on the sofa. He looked peaceful and relaxed.

'I don't understand you,' I said. 'You don't seem at all worried about Meg, yet only a little while before I went out you agreed with me that she might be in danger. What's happened to you? Don't you care?'

'I care to the extent that I've taken steps to protect her,' he said. 'I thought that was advisable.'

'I don't understand,' I repeated. 'What steps could you take?'

'I removed her from the scene, that's all.'

'You don't make sense.'

'It's quite simple,' he said. 'I sent her to London. To Little Carbery Street, to be exact.'

'To the flat? How on earth did you induce her to go there?'

'It just happens she has a certain regard for me and was ready to listen to my advice. I know you find it astonishing that anyone should have any regard for me and take me seriously, but that very nice and intelligent young woman thinks quite a lot of me. And that's a wonderfully refreshing feeling, let me tell you, after the treatment I usually get. I'd flourish on a bit more of it.'

'But when did you see her?' I asked.

'Just after you went out shopping. She came here on purpose to consult me on what she ought to do. She said she'd been walking about, trying to make up her own mind, then thought I was the kind of person who might be able to help her. It was just as we guessed. The

201

Bodwells told her about having witnessed a will and it had dawned on her all of a sudden that that conflicted with her beloved Huddleston's story that he'd been asked to the house by Mrs Arliss to destroy a will. It hadn't occurred to her that she might be in any danger because of her knowledge, but she was very upset, thinking that perhaps it was her duty to tell the police what she knew, yet dreading the thought of getting Huddleston into trouble. She's a very nice girl, Virginia, extremely honest, loyal and sensitive. I wish there were more like her.'

'But why didn't you advise her to go to the police?' I asked. 'Her story about the will would back up yours. It wouldn't be just your word against Patrick's any more.'

He gave a sigh. 'You ask so many questions.'

'Well, why didn't you send her to them?'

'As a matter of fact, I rather doubted, when it came to the point, if she'd go.'

'So you terrified her into hiding in Little Carbery Street.'

'I did nothing of the kind. I merely suggested she might like some peace and quiet in which to sort out her problems. She seemed very grateful. It's true I pointed out she might be in some slight danger staying here if she told anyone else what she knew, but I was very careful not to scare her too much.'

'Only enough to send her in a blind panic to London without even a toothbrush.'

'D'you know, I sometimes think the importance of toothbrushes is overrated,' he said.

'Did you give her a key to the flat?'

'Of course.'

I was puzzled by his expression. There was a look of contentment about it, a kind of calm, which generally meant that he was lost in some fantasy that particularly pleased him. Suddenly I felt suspicious.

'Felix, did any of this really happen?' I asked.

'All of it,' he said.

'She came here to consult you, she told you what the Bodwells said about witnessing a will and you sent her off to London?'

'Isn't that what I said?'

I looked at my watch. 'She hasn't had time to get to the flat yet, but when she has I'll telephone and find out what she has to say about it.'

'I was going to suggest that myself,' he said. 'She likes you. She'll be glad to hear from you. It'll reassure her.'

That sounded as if he really had sent her to the flat. But I was still puzzled by his look of satisfaction. He was keeping something from me, I felt sure, though whether it was something that Meg had told him or something that he had done I did not know. But questioning would get me nowhere, so I left him in peace and went to the kitchen to unpack my shopping basket. I had just begun when the doorbell rang.

It was Superintendent Chance, accompanied by the young sergeant.

The sergeant gave me a smile, so cheerful that it looked as if he was really glad to see me. Mr Chance gave me a sombre greeting. His footsteps dragged. He seemed to feel that there was no point in hurrying about a not very important matter.

I took the two of them into the sitting-room, where Felix, on the sofa, appeared to have fallen asleep. But he had merely closed his eyes and as soon as the detectives entered, they sprang open, bright, shrewd and somehow prepared for the interview ahead. Getting quickly to his feet, he urged the two men to sit down and asked them if they felt it was too early for a drink. They refused the drink, but accepted chairs, though Mr Chance seemed to do this with a kind of reluctance, as if he felt it made him run the risk of being brought into a social relationship with Felix and me, which he did not in the least desire.

'There are just one or two questions I'd like to ask you,' he said. 'I won't take up much of your time. It's just to check up on one or two things you told Sergeant Peabody this morning. I want to be sure about the time the Bodwells left London after Mrs Freer's visit. Can you tell me that?'

'I think I told the sergeant it was about nine

o'clock,' Felix said.

'Are you still sure about that? You haven't had any second thoughts on the matter?'

'No, it was just around nine or soon after,' Felix answered.

'It couldn't have been earlier?'

'Oh no, give or take a few minutes.'

'A pity,' Mr Chance said in the resigned tone of someone who is used to disappointment in his work. 'You're quite sure of that, now?'

'Perfectly sure.'

'Then there's the question of why they came here. Have you had any ideas about that since you talked to Sergeant Peabody this morning?'

Without any hesitation, Felix shook his head. His face was bland and co-operative.

'Not any at all, I'm afraid.'

'But you knew them well.'

'I thought I did.'

'Did they never suggest to you that they had a hold on somebody here, which might make it worth their while to come back to see what they could make out of it before they set off to look for a new job?'

'No,' Felix said. 'If that's what they did, they never said anything about it to me.'

I almost protested. What about the will that they had witnessed that probably had given them a hold on Patrick, I wanted to ask. But just as I was going to do it, I realized that I had never heard anything about that will except from Felix and it was always possible that it

205

was one of his inventions. A rather complicated invention, even for him, but still not guaranteed truth. And it was plain that he had no intention of mentioning the will himself at the moment. I did not know his reason for this, but I knew that if I said anything about it, he was capable of contradicting me.

'I hadn't thought of it before,' he went on, looking thoughtful and earnestly helpful, 'but now you mention it, it does seem to me possible they had a hold of some sort on Mr Tustin. But you'll have thought of that yourselves.'

'You mean that they may have seen him taking the miniatures,' Mr Chance said.

'It's quite likely, isn't it? They were in the house when he took them.'

'It's possible, yes.' But Mr Chance did not sound enthusiastic. 'However, I'm sure Mr Tustin would never have allowed himself to be blackmailed over such a thing. By the time the Bodwells came here, he knew the miniatures belonged to him and that he hadn't committed any offence, even if he'd intended to originally.'

'But did the Bodwells know that?' Felix asked. 'Mightn't they have come on the chance of screwing just a bit of cash out of him? They'd have known Mr Tustin was a very worthy man, the kind who's very sensitive about his reputation. I can easily imagine him

206

being willing to pay some small amount for their silence.'

'Hm. Yes. Well.' Mr Chance seemed to be thinking this over, though with very little expression on his face to show what he thought of it. 'But you're certain the Bodwells didn't leave London before nine o'clock?'

Felix nodded gravely. 'I'm sorry I can't be more helpful.'

He saw the two detectives to the door.

When he came back into the room, I said, 'Felix, the Bodwells never said anything to you about having seen Nigel take the miniatures, did they?'

'No,' he said.

'Then why try to drag poor old Nigel into things all of a sudden?'

'I just didn't want to be completely disobliging. I felt I ought to offer them something. And it's not a bad theory, is it?'

'At least you didn't actually suggest he murdered Imogen, though you came rather near it.'

'We aren't certain he didn't, are we, even if we haven't unearthed a motive for him? But that may come yet.'

'Tell me, why is Mr Chance so determined to get you to say that the Bodwells left London before nine o'clock?'

'Oh, that's obvious.' Felix dropped into his usual sprawl on the sofa. 'Suppose they had a hold on someone here, as in fact we know they had a hold on Huddleston, and suppose they wanted to get some money out of him, it isn't unlikely they'd have telephoned beforehand to make sure he had the money and to arrange a meeting. And suppose Huddleston told them to meet him in the Arliss house, got hold of the gun, shot them in the car as soon as they arrived, drove them to Deepstead and dumped them and then threw the gun away. Imogen, of course, would have had to be in on it too, because she'd have had to follow in Huddleston's car to pick him up when he got out of the Bodwells' and bring him back. And then he might have got scared of her knowing what she did. He may just have been afraid that she wouldn't be able to help talking if any pressure was put on her. So he killed her too. In other words, the Bodwells weren't killed because they saw Imogen's murder, but she was killed because she saw theirs. Chance thinks it all fits together nicely.'

'But the time element makes it impossible.'

'Absolutely. If the Bodwells didn't leave London before nine o'clock, they couldn't have got here before ten-fifteen at the earliest. And they'd have had to be killed, driven the ten miles to Deepstead and Imogen and Huddleston would have had to get back to the house before ten-forty-five, when the tree crashed. They couldn't have done it.'

'Couldn't they just have done it if they'd driven fast?'

'Along narrow lanes, with two dead bodies in the car? They'd have gone quite slowly, I'm certain, not wanting to draw attention to themselves. And they didn't know the tree was going to crash. They didn't know there was any need to hurry.'

'Yes, I see.' But I was impressed by the ingenuity of his theory and did not want to part with it immediately. 'When did you think all this out?'

'When Chance kept harping on the time the Bodwells left London. I saw at once what he was getting at and I found it very tempting to tell him they left half an hour or so before they did, because he'd have been so pleased.'

'Actually it doesn't have to have been Patrick and Imogen,' I said. 'It could have been Meg and Paul.'

'Only neither of them has a car, so the one who followed would have had to have taken the Rolls and that would have been a little bit conspicuous. Or they could have taken Imogen's car, as she was out in Huddleston's, but she might have come back before them and spotted it was gone. It's true their only alibi is that they went to the cinema together, which is really no alibi at all, whereas Huddleston and Imogen were at the Rose and Crown, where they'll be remembered.'

'I suppose Mr Chance has checked that—I mean, that they didn't leave earlier than Patrick said.'

'I wonder . . .' He paused, then swung his feet to the ground and stood up. 'D'you know, I think I'll check that myself. I'll go along and have a chat with the waiter. I suppose that means I'll have to have a drink. Can I borrow a little money? I forgot all about going to the bank today, but I'll go tomorrow, I promise.'

I gave him some money and he went out.

It was only after he had gone that it dawned on me what the fantasy was that he was enjoying. He was seeing himself as the great detective. He had been playing the part, I realized, ever since the morning. His unwillingness to tell the police any of his theories was not because he had anything to hide, or because he was afraid that they would not believe him, but was simply because he wanted to solve the crime himself.

His sending Meg to London fitted in with this. At least one great detective of fiction had had a habit of hiding important witnesses in obscure hotels until they could be produced with the maximum amount of drama. Only those witnesses, I remembered, had had an unfortunate way of disappearing just when they were most needed. That was part of the pattern.

That was a worrying thought. But it was not one that I took particularly seriously, because Meg, after all, did not know the role that she was playing in Felix's daydream and so would not necessarily stick to its rules.

All the same, I wished that he had sent her to the police instead of to the flat, for what could she do there beyond waste some time until she made up her mind to tell the police about the will that the Bodwells had witnessed, which was what she would have to do ultimately, however much she wanted to protect Patrick. Her disappearance in itself would tell the police that she was concealing something and once they were sure of that it would not take them long to get it out of her. She was not someone who would stand up well under stress. Her breaking-point would come early. Of course they would have to find her first, but I did not think that they would find that very difficult. It was a pity all round that the great detective had been so irresponsible.

He returned in about an hour's time, looking solemn and abstracted. But he had nothing much to tell me except that Patrick and Imogen had been in the Rose and Crown on the evening of the murder, as Patrick had said, until about ten-fifteen. Therefore the possibility that he had murdered the Bodwells after that, driven their bodies to Deepstead, then got back to the Arliss house before the tree crashed, could be ruled out completely.

'I never thought otherwise,' Felix said, 'but one must be thorough. Now why don't you ring up the flat and see if Meg's all right?'

I had been just about to do that. Picking up the telephone, I dialled and heard it ring about ten times before I put it down again.

'She hasn't got there yet,' I said.

He frowned. 'But she must have. She's had lots of time.'

'Perhaps she thought of something else she wanted to do first,' I said.

'I suppose she must have. We'll try again later. Now what are we going to eat? Shall I cook it or will you?'

'It's only chops,' I said. 'I'll do it.'

He seemed relieved, as if he had too much on his mind to be able to concentrate on cooking. Yet he lurked about the kitchen, getting in my way, as I got ahead with it. Mostly he was silent, sipping one of his weak whiskies, but he seemed to want an audience for his deep thoughtfulness.

'No,' he muttered presently as the chops began to sizzle, 'that won't do.'

'Has some brilliant idea turned out to have a hole in it?' I asked. 'You really ought to be drinking bourbon, you know.'

He missed the point. 'I don't know what you're talking about. I never touch it. What I've been turning over in my mind is the idea that Huddleston might have made an appointment to meet the Bodwells at Deepstead *before* going to the Rose and Crown. It didn't occur to me to check the time he and Imogen got there, but only the time they left. And the Bodwells could have got to Deepstead sooner than they could have to

Allingford, so that would have given them a bit of extra time after leaving London. But apart from the fact that the police will have checked Huddleston's alibi more thoroughly than I did, the Bodwells would never have agreed to a meeting in an out of the way place like that lane. They were professionals. They'd never have made a blunder like that. But the trouble is, the only other motive I've been able to think of for Huddleston murdering Imogen is so damned complicated, isn't it? I mean her threatening to disclose his fiddling with the will. I don't like it. I believe in simple ideas.'

'No one else seems to have any motive at all,' I said.

'Except Meg. And even if she could brain Imogen with a shovel, I'd be surprised if she knows how to use a gun.'

'What about Paul then?' I suggested. 'Suppose he loves Meg so much, he had a rush of self-sacrifice to the head and killed Imogen so that Meg could marry Patrick and live happily ever after. Isn't that beautiful and simple?'

'I'm serious,' he said reprovingly.

'I can see that,' I said, 'but it's so odd, seeing you on the side of the angels for once, that I'm rather bewildered by it.'

'It's a challenge to the imagination,' he replied. 'That's why I find it so absorbing.'

'Like trying to find a way of travelling on the Underground without paying the full fare,' I said. 'I remember how you were utterly absorbed in thinking out how to do that, and in the end, when you found a way, it took far more effort than just paying what you were supposed to. It must often be very hard work, being crooked.'

'I wasn't being crooked, I was just trying to beat the system,' he said. 'Those chops smell very good.'

'We may as well eat in here.' I took knives and forks from a drawer and laid them on the kitchen table. 'And afterwards I'll ring Meg again and see if she's got to the flat yet. But what do we do if she hasn't?'

'She must be there by now,' he said.

'But if she isn't?'

'She will be. Don't worry. She wanted to go there. She was pleased when I suggested it. The only thing is . . .' He paused.

'Yes?'

'Did she tell anyone else she was going there before she left? No, I'm sure she wouldn't have. She didn't want anyone to know where she was going. It's all right, she'll be there by now.'

But when I dialled the flat again about half an hour later, the telephone rang on and on as before and there was still no answer.

At last Felix showed signs of being worried.

'She promised me she wouldn't go out or open the door to anyone,' he said. 'I told her there was food in the fridge and I'd get in touch with her tomorrow.'

'Tomorrow?' I said. 'How's the situation going to have changed by tomorrow? Won't she be in just the same danger as she is today? If there was any point in your sending her to London, hadn't she better stay there?'

'But is she there? Or did she change her mind and not go at all? Or—was she stopped?'

'Perhaps she just went home,' I said. 'Perhaps she calmed down after talking to you and just went home. I think I'll ring up the house and ask if she's there.'

'Yes,' he said, 'do that.'

He was impatient and anxious.

I dialled the Arliss number and almost immediately Paul replied. He must have been waiting by the telephone, hoping that it would ring. But as soon as I spoke I heard him draw his breath in sharply before forcing himself to say in a relatively calm tone, 'Oh, it's you, Virginia.'

'Yes. Is Meg there?' I asked.

'No, she isn't,' he answered.

'We've been wondering about her ever since she came here,' I said. 'Do you know where she is?'

His voice went up sharply. 'I don't and I'm worried as hell. It's so unlike her. I mean, just to disappear before lunch without a word to anyone. It's true we had a sort of quarrel before she left and at first I thought that was why she'd gone and that she'd come back

215

presently when she'd got over it, but she hasn't come back or even telephoned and I don't know what to do.'

'What was the quarrel about?' I asked.

'Nothing much. I only said something mildly disparaging about Patrick, something about what a fool he must have been, considering he was Aunt Evelyn's solicitor, not to have found out she hadn't any money to leave, and Meg flew into a rage at my saying anything critical of him. It's awful, isn't it, what he means to her even now she knows all about him and Imogen? She must know she doesn't mean anything to him.'

'Have you tried telephoning him to ask if he's seen her?' I asked.

'Yes, I tried him at his office and then later on at his home and he said he didn't know anything about her. He acted worried, but I don't think he really cared.'

'Have you telephoned the police?'

'Not yet. I didn't want her to feel she was being hounded, if all she wanted was some time to herself. But now it's so late, perhaps I ought to do that. What do you think?'

I was just going to say that I thought he should when Felix took the telephone out of my hand. He had been standing close to me and had overheard most of what Paul had said.

'I shouldn't go to the police yet, Paul,' he said. 'Give me a little time. I think I may be able to find her and she'll probably prefer that

216

to having the police track her down.'

'Do you know where she is then?' Paul asked.

'I've a good idea,' Felix answered.

I wanted to snatch the telephone and tell Paul to take no notice of what Felix had said, but he fended me off with one arm.

'If I'm wrong, I'll telephone again in a little while,' he said, 'and you can go to the police then.' He put the telephone down.

'What ever made you talk to the poor boy like that?' I asked angrily. 'He's going crazy with worry and you haven't any idea where Meg is, now that you know she isn't in the flat.'

'But I have,' Felix said. 'It came to me while you were talking. Come along, let's go and get her.' He went to the door. I did not move. 'Where is she?' I asked.

'With Huddleston.'

'But he said he hadn't seen her.'

'Does he have to have been speaking the truth?'

'Why d'you think she's with him?'

'Because she can't keep away from him. And she's come to the conclusion, I feel fairly sure now, that if she tells him what she suspects about the will he'll be able to explain it away. Come along, I don't think we should waste time.'

There was something in his tone that gave me a shiver. Felix, with his strange gift of intuition that made him such a competent con man, was often right about people where I went hopelessly wrong. I went with him, although I only half-believed him.

We took his car and he drove. It was not yet fully dark out of doors, but that early dusk which is the most deceptive light in the day, when shadows look solid and solid things insubstantial. The ambiguity of that half-light increased my feeling of tension. Once or twice I spoke to Felix, but he did not answer. He looked as if he were concentrating entirely on his driving. But this was a look which I knew was as deceptive as the blurred twilight through which he was taking me. He could drive excellently with only a fraction of his mind on the job. His concentration now was either acting, part of his role of great detective, or else he was really concentrating on something about which he had said nothing to me so far.

We drove around the edge of the market place and on into one of the streets that led out of it towards the block of flats where Patrick lived. He lived alone there, with a woman coming in in the mornings to do his cleaning. He ate most of his meals out in the various restaurants of the town. He was not domesticated, like Felix, and able to look after himself. As we turned into the drive up to the flats, a pseudo-Georgian block in red brick, I felt sure that we should find that he was out now, still having dinner somewhere, and that our drive would turn out to have been for nothing.

But just as Felix was turning into an empty space in the car-park in front of the flats, two figures emerged from the entrance, pausing there for a moment under the lights. They were Meg and Patrick. He was holding her by an elbow and they appeared to be talking earnestly. Then they walked on across the drive towards one of the cars a little way ahead of us.

Felix rapidly backed out of the space that he had started to enter.

'He's got his car,' he said. 'How did he get it out past the tree?'

'It isn't his car,' I said. 'He must have hired it.'

I started to get out of the car, meaning to call out to Meg.

Felix dragged me back, leaning across me to slam the door shut.

'No, not now,' he said. 'We follow them.'

CHAPTER TEN

It was not long before we realized where the car ahead of us was going.

'He's taking her home,' I said.

'Good,' Felix said. 'That's what I hoped.'

'Then you never believed she was in danger from him.'

'As to that, it's better to be safe than sorry.'

'Or did you think he might be in danger from her?'

'Even that wasn't impossible,' he said. 'I know I told you I'd be surprised if she knew how to use a gun, but for all I know she was weaned on one. Some parents teach their children extraordinary things.'

'Anyway, she doesn't seem to have taken you very seriously when you advised her to go to London.'

'No, I suppose she never meant to go. Talking to me just cleared her mind up for her somehow. She realized that what she wanted most was to give Huddleston a chance to persuade her of his basic integrity. And from the look of things, he's succeeded.'

Patrick's hired car stopped at some traffic lights. Felix pulled in behind him. It was dark by now and there was nothing to be seen of the two people in the car ahead of us but the silhouettes of their heads against the light of the street lamps. Patrick did not glance behind him or show any awareness of being followed. If he knew that he was, he was not disturbed by it.

When the traffic lights changed, he drove straight on and Felix stayed on his tail. I asked him why he was doing that instead of returning to Ellsworthy Street, but he did not answer and I did not repeat the question. His features were set once more in a look of deep concentration, and I knew that it would be useless to try to find out what he was thinking about. It might even be nothing at all, though he would never admit it. He slowed down when Patrick stopped at Mrs Arliss's gate, I supposed to see if he and Meg were going into the house, or if he was only dropping her off there, but when they both got out of the car and started up the drive, Felix drove his car up close behind Patrick's and got out too.

'Come along,' he said as I joined him on the pavement, 'it's time this mess got cleared up, or God knows what will happen next.'

'Are you going to clear it up?' I asked.

'Why not?' He started walking up the drive. 'I've been fairly sure for some time what must have happened, but I couldn't think how to handle it. If I'd gone about it the wrong way, it could just have been a way of warning the murderer. And I don't want him to get away with it. I'm not normally a vindictive man, as you know, and also I'm very doubtful of the value of punishment as such, but the Bodwells, if you don't mind my repeating myself, were my friends and I feel I owe it to them to expose their murderer. Once I've done that, the police can take over.'

'You don't think it would be better if they took over straight away?' I said. 'I mean, if you know something that you could tell them.'

We left the drive and walked across the lawn, skirting the fallen tree.

'I've certain advantages that are denied to them,' he said, 'as you will see.'

There was an unfamiliar grimness in his voice that puzzled me. Had he really some plan in his head, I wondered, that would unmask a murderer, or was it all part of a charade that he would drop as soon as we entered the house? We were both silent as we went up to it and he rang the doorbell.

Meg opened the door. From the way that Felix smiled at her, all his grimness disappearing, I thought my guess that it had been one of his charades must have been correct. Meg, as she smiled back, looked embarrassed, her pale cheeks flushing a little.

'You see, I didn't go to London after all,' she said. 'I must give you back your key. I feel rather awful about it, because you were so understanding, but just talking things over with you helped a lot and when I left you I began to feel there was really no need to run away and hide. All I wanted was the courage to have things out with Patrick. So I went for a long bus ride to fill in the time till I knew he'd be home from the office, then went to see him and told him all my worries. And he can explain everything. Isn't it wonderful? I need never have worried at all. I'm feeling such a fool now to have had the suspicions of him that I did. But come in and get him to explain it to you himself. He was just going to tell the others.'

She led the way into the drawing-room.

That room had always oppressed me. It was a room for formal gatherings of people who did not much like one another. No one had thought of drawing the curtains and the long, blank panes of the sash windows were chilly expanses of blackness, which gave back reflections of the room in an eerie way. An excellent room, it might be, in which to conduct an inquest, if that was what Felix seriously had in mind, but I could not believe any longer that this was what he intended. He looked friendly and mildly diffident, as if he were not sure of his welcome here, and not at all as if he had come to make accusations.

Nigel, Paul and Patrick were in the room, Nigel standing on the hearth-rug with his back to the empty fireplace, Paul scrambling up from a small, hard-looking sofa, Patrick leaning on the back of a chair, holding it with both hands, as if it were a rostrum and he was about to make a speech, as indeed he was. He let our arrival delay him only for a moment.

'I want to make a confession,' he said. 'Perhaps I should have done it sooner, but I didn't think the matter was of any great importance till Meg made me understand how certain actions of mine could be misunderstood. So I'll get ahead with it now, if you don't mind. It concerns the last will and testament of Mrs Arliss.' He smiled at his audience, with no intention, plainly, of being taken too seriously.

Paul had sat down again and Meg had sat down beside him. Felix had gone to one of the tall windows and was standing gazing out at the blackness of the garden with his back to the room. He seemed to be studying his own reflection in the glass rather than listening to Patrick. I sat down on one of the small Victorian chairs and kept my eyes on Patrick's face as he went on talking. Not that it told me much. He was not looking at us as if we were friends, but rather as if we were a group of clients whom he did not know very well but whom it was his professional duty to reassure.

'The fact is,' he said in his light, amiable voice, 'when Mrs Arliss sent for me a few days before her death, it wasn't merely to have me destroy her last will, but to make a new one. A most extraordinary will. Of course, I didn't know at the time that she'd no money to leave and I don't think she knew it herself by then. She started instructing me to leave vast legacies to servants who'd left her years ago. In one or two cases, I even happened to know, they were dead. If any money had gone to them it would actually have been inherited by their relations, whom Mrs Arliss didn't even know existed. Then she left a great sum of money to endow a hospital in Allingford which was to be called after her, which seemed very peculiar to me when it dawned on me that the amount she was leaving for this project was even more than I thought she still possessed. Then she wanted a monument to her husband to be erected in the market place here. I think it was that that made me realize what was happening. The poor woman was completely out of her mind. And as you can imagine, I was left with a very tricky problem to handle. I had to make up my mind very quickly what to do. Should I try to argue her out of going on with this will that she seemed intent on making? Should I protest and remind her that she had relations to care for? Naturally, that was my first impulse. But honestly, I didn't think it would do any good. The only thing she could think of just then was how to perpetuate the name of Arliss in Allingford. Horribly sad in a woman who'd always been as astute and realistic as she had.'

He coughed slightly, as if to apologize for his momentary lapse into sentiment.

'Then there was the alternative of letting her sign the will,' he went on, 'then leaving it

225

to Imogen and Nigel to contest it after she was dead. They wouldn't have had much difficulty in doing that, I was fairly sure, and perhaps that's what I ought to have done. But there was something so much easier to do than that, which was going to save everyone trouble. It was simply to destroy the will without telling anyone anything about it. And that's what I did. I did it out of friendship, I do hope you'll understand that. I didn't stand to gain anything by it myself, I only wanted to save the family a tedious legal action. And none of you need have known anything about the matter if Mrs Arliss hadn't been sufficiently on the spot to know that she had to have her signature witnessed and insisted on calling in the Bodwells to do it. At the time that didn't worry me much. I only knew them as excellent servants, I didn't know that they ran a side-line in blackmail. But when Mrs Arliss died and they heard that her will had been made a year ago, they grasped at once what I'd done and I suppose it was to squeeze something out of me for their silence that they came down here the night before last. But unluckily for them, they missed me. If they went to my flat first, they may have heard from the porter that I'd gone out with Miss Dale and have thought that meant I'd come here. And in fact we'd got back here and I'd left already by the time the Bodwells arrived and what they blundered into was Imogen's murder. But that's another story.

226

What I want you to understand are all the facts about the will I destroyed, which Meg found out about from the Bodwells, though she misunderstood my motives. I think I've been able to reassure her that they weren't as bad as she thought they were and I hope the rest of you will also forgive me for having been so irresponsible when I was only trying to help you.'

He did not quite make a bow when his speech ended, but he looked as if he was expecting applause.

Nigel gave an embarrassed cough and shifted uneasily from one foot to the other. Paul put an arm round Meg and drew her closer to him. She rested against him as if she found this a comfortable arrangement. Felix turned from the window, lighting a cigarette as he did so, and gave Patrick a long, thoughtful look.

'That's a nice story,' Felix said. 'Artistic. I like it. It covers the facts beautifully. Unfortunately I don't believe a word of it.'

Patrick flushed a deep red. 'What do you mean?'

'It's quite simple,' Felix said. 'The Bodwells told me Mrs Arliss was mentally perfectly normal right up to the time of her second stroke. Also, she's known to have said she wanted to do the right thing by Imogen. So if we assume that she was perfectly well aware that she hadn't any money to leave, it seems obvious that what she did in that last will was to leave the only valuable thing she possessed, the miniatures, to Imogen, and the almost non-existent residue to Nigel. But you didn't know there wasn't any money, so you destroyed that will, wanting Imogen to inherit what you believed was great wealth, as she would have under an earlier one. It wasn't an unreasonable thing to do, as you hoped to marry her, but you let Imogen know what you'd done, which wasn't very clever, because when you tried to call the marriage off, she held her knowledge over your head, saying that if you didn't marry her, she'd expose you. At which point you went berserk and bashed her skull in with the copper shovel. And that's what the Bodwells saw through the window.'

The redness of Patrick's face faded, leaving his dark skin almost yellow.

'You're crazy,' he said. 'Imogen and I agreed to marry that evening. We wanted to marry. The money didn't matter.'

'But I'm right about the will,' Felix said. 'All that stuff about the Evelyn Arliss Hospital and so on—you made that up to conceal the fact that the real reason why you destroyed that last will was that you believed you were making Imogen a rich woman.'

'Suppose that's so,' Patrick said, his tone growing blustering, 'not that I admit it, but even if it were so, does it mean I murdered Imogen? Good God, man, I was in love with

228

her! I've been in love with her for years.'

Felix looked resigned. 'Then you don't like my theory. To be honest, I talked it over with Virginia and we're neither of us too sold on it ourselves. Imogen had got on for a good long time without marrying. It wouldn't have worried her too much to go on for a while longer. But I've lots of theories more. The one about Nigel, for instance.'

Nigel gave a start. His thoughts seemed to have wandered. His eyes were on the miniatures, which were his only because of Patrick's miscalculation.

'I beg your pardon,' he said. 'Did you say something to me?'

'I'm only suggesting you may have murdered Imogen and the Bodwells,' Felix said.

'Good heavens!'

'It isn't at all a bad theory,' Felix went on. 'If the Bodwells saw you take the miniatures and came down here to threaten you and you shot them and drove them off to Deepstead and walked back and Imogen saw you, soaking wet when you got back into the house, you might well have killed her to silence her.'

'Yes,' Nigel said heavily. 'Yes, I see. Possible, almost. And naturally I'd have cleaned the mud off my shoes the next morning, shouldn't I? That's the sort of thing I shouldn't have been careless about. The only thing is, my behaviour doesn't seem to me to

229

have been very rational and on the whole, I'm not an irrational man. I have lapses, I admit, of the kind I had when I took the miniatures, but why should I be so afraid of what the Bodwells could reveal about that when I'd already returned the miniatures to myself? They might have thought they had some power over me and come here to see what they could get out of it, but I'm sure we could have settled the whole matter in a few minutes of reasonable talk. And they'd only to see the miniatures back on the wall to realize there was nothing in it for them.'

'I was afraid you'd think of that,' Felix said. 'You're perfectly right, of course. The Bodwells could have made you look ridiculous, but you'd have had to be a pathological case to have found that an adequate motive for murder. Not that our murderer isn't a pathological case. I'm sure he is. Most murderers are, at least in our society at the present time. In some societies and in some periods of history, as in wartime, when killing is actively encouraged, it can become a perfectly normal activity. But in our little circle you can hardly regard it as sane.'

'You say, "he",' Meg interrupted. 'Haven't you a theory about me?'

'Well, as a matter of fact, I have,' Felix replied good-naturedly, as if he thought that it would please her not to be left out. 'You've an excellent motive for the murder of Imogen, if

230

you don't mind my referring to it. You felt extremely jealous, didn't you, when you heard of the affair between her and Huddleston? And you're quite strong enough to have killed her with the shovel, and for all I know, you may be highly trained in using a gun, so it's possible you could have killed the Bodwells—'

'This is appalling!' Patrick broke in angrily. 'I won't listen to any more of it. Meg wouldn't hurt a fly. And as for her jealousy, well, I'd like to think I could mean as much to her as that, but I don't think for a moment I do.'

'You're being modest,' Felix said. 'I'm right about that, as far as it goes, aren't I, Meg?'

She gave Patrick a curiously apologetic smile. 'I suppose so. I rather lost my head for a time, I'm afraid. But you needn't worry, Patrick. I don't mind talking about it now, because I've come to my senses about it. I know I was awfully stupid. It wasn't in the least your fault. And it's all over now, in fact, in a funny way, I can't even quite remember what I thought I felt. You must think I'm very childish.'

'But just as a matter of interest,' Felix said, 'do you know how to use a gun?'

'No, she said, 'I've never even handled one.'

'Can you drive a car?'

She looked puzzled. 'No.'

'You've never driven one?'

'No.'

'You've never held a driving licence?'

'Never.'

Felix smiled at her benignly. 'Well, there you are then. That's a fact that can be proved, which is lucky for you, because the murderer drove the Bodwells to Deepstead and negative things on the whole are hard to prove. It could be quite hard to prove that you can't shoot, or that you couldn't kill anyone with a shovel, or that you aren't in love with Patrick any more. But the police can easily find out if you ever passed a driving test and held a driving licence. You're sure you're telling me the truth about that now, are you, because if you aren't, the police will soon get on to it?'

No one could sound sterner than Felix about the necessity of other people telling the truth.

Meg gave her head a little shake. 'I feel rather a fool about it actually, but I've never learnt to drive. I've never been able to afford a car of my own, so it didn't seem important.'

'That's what I thought,' Felix said, 'but I wanted to be sure. So that leaves Paul.'

All the kindliness suddenly left his face. The touch of theatricality with which he had been talking, the pretence of being a great detective, also vanished. It was one of the rare moments when Felix was nothing but himself. He looked several years older than he usually did, as if his charming air of youthfulness had never been anything but make-believe. The shrewd, hard gaze of an experienced, ageing man looked from under his drooping eyelids at the apparently puzzled Paul.

'You've always been my favourite suspect,' Felix said, 'because I like simple ideas and your motive for killing Imogen was far the simplest. You did it for her money, didn't you?'

Paul's face, with the ruddy cheeks that could look so like Imogen's, darkened.

'I don't know what you're talking about,' he said. 'She hadn't any money.'

'But she had,' Felix said. 'From her own point of view she may have been a poor woman, but a good many people would have thought her a rich one. She'd a private income, which may not have been adequate for her own needs, but which could have looked quite tempting to you, even allowing for death duties. And she'd a delightful small Regency house in Hampstead. How much is that worth, do you think? Eighty or ninety thousand? It was partly so that she could keep that house that she wanted money so badly from Mrs Arliss. I heard her say that as there wasn't any, she'd probably have to sell it and go to live in a flat in the suburbs. And you were her sole heir, weren't you? You could count on inheriting everything from her—until she told you that she was going to marry Patrick.'

Paul got up abruptly. His face and his neck were red. 'If you're serious . . .'

'Why shouldn't I be?' Felix asked. 'It's what happened, isn't it? She'd been good to you

233

when you were a boy and looked after you and you'd always been able to go to her for money when you wanted it. Anyway, until you got a job and went to live in a flat of your own. Was that because she'd got tired of looking after you and told you to stand on your own feet and did you bear her a grudge because of it? Whether or not that's how it was, you still took it for granted she'd leave everything she had to you. But that evening, when you and Meg got in from the cinema, Imogen told you she was going to marry Huddleston. I'm not certain exactly how it happened, but I think you and Meg came in together, went upstairs, said good night and went to your rooms, then something made you come downstairs again. Perhaps you'd seen a light under the door of this room and guessed that Imogen was still up and you wanted a chat with her. Anyway, you found her and she told you that she and Huddleston had decided to get married. She was all happiness, wasn't she, because she'd discovered he wanted to marry her although, from her own point of view, she hadn't any money? And you realized she'd soon be making a will, leaving everything to him—he wouldn't have let her forget about doing that, I imagine—and perhaps she taunted you because you weren't going to get anything out of her. I can easily see her doing that. She could be very cruel when she chose. And in your fury and disappointment, you killed her.

And then you saw the Bodwells at the window.'

Paul took a step towards Felix, then checked himself, but I was suddenly aware how young and strong and menacing he looked and how small Felix seemed, facing him. Paul, however, laughed.

'You're making this up as you go along,' he said, 'as you're so fond of doing. But even you can't pretend you've a shadow of proof of it.'

'But I have,' Felix said.

Paul shook his head, still smiling, though the smile had a rather fixed look, as if it had been painted on to his face.

'It's all right, we all found out long ago what lies you tell,' he said. 'But it's not a very good joke.'

'It's no joke,' Felix said. 'Ask Meg. Ask her what she came to talk to me about this afternoon. When she didn't get your lunch and disappeared, she came to see me, did you know that? And do you know the reason? You and she had been out shopping yesterday morning and walking down the drive you both got your shoes muddy and she hadn't given that a second thought until the police came here, wanting to see all your shoes. Then she remembered, your shoes were muddy already when you started out from the house to go shopping, not only when you got back. And she didn't know what to do, because she's fond of you and didn't want to make unnecessary

235

trouble for you, but at the same time she's a law-abiding, conscientious girl and she doesn't like murder. So she came to talk it over with me, because she felt sure of my sympathy—'

'But I never . . .' Meg interrupted, then stopped, one hand going to her mouth as she looked distractedly from Felix to Paul.

'You did come to see me, didn't you, Meg?' Felix asked gently.

'Oh yes,' she said, 'but I didn't—I mean, I never . . .' She left it hanging, one of her unfinished sentences.

'You didn't think it was a really serious matter,' Felix ended it for her, not, I thought, as she had intended. 'Indeed, why should you? You just wanted a little reassurance. However, that isn't the only proof I've got.'

'It isn't a proof at all,' Paul said. 'If you're trying to scare me, you'll have to do better than that. Meg, there isn't a word of truth in this, is there? You didn't start worrying about those shoes.'

She was looking at Felix with a hypnotized stare and did not answer.

'Actually, I've a very much better proof,' he said in a soft voice which sent a prickle up my spine, it sounded so sinister. 'I've some direct evidence. It happens that I saw you shoot the Bodwells. That shakes you, doesn't it? I'd hoped I'd never have to say it. I didn't want to get mixed up in the affair any more than I could help. I hoped the police would solve the

236

murders without any help from me. You see, I came down with the Bodwells when they came here to try to raise a little ready cash from Huddleston. I didn't come into the house with them, because I didn't want him to know I was in on the deal. If he had known it might have been embarrassing for Virginia. I keep embarrassing Virginia, though I always do my best to avoid it. The Bodwells left their car outside the gate and walked up the drive and I waited in the car. Then after a time I heard them coming back and they were talking to someone, so in case it was someone I didn't want to meet, I got out of the car and stepped back into the shadows, where I wouldn't be seen. And it was you, Paul. You were begging and imploring them not to tell anyone about something or other—I didn't know what it was at the time, of course, but it was the murder of Imogen, wasn't it?—and you were promising to send them more money as soon as you could lay your hands on it. And then, as the three of you were standing by the car, you took a gun out of your pocket and cold-bloodedly shot them. Then you bundled their bodies into the car. I don't think Rita died immediately. I heard her moan. And then you drove off. You must have had a long, wet walk back after leaving the car at Deepstead, but you're young and energetic. It wouldn't have been too much for you. And I suppose there's an electric fire in your bedroom, so that you could dry your clothes off during the night.' Paul raised clenched fists.

'It's all lies, all lies!' he shouted. 'You couldn't have been there. She didn't—'

He stopped, realizing what he had nearly said. Then he launched himself at Felix.

It was Nigel who astonished me then. If he had not acted as he did, I think Paul might have murdered Felix. But stiff, middle-aged, pompous as Nigel was, it was evident that once upon a time he had been trained in unarmed combat. Unfortunately, he hurt his back that evening and afterwards had a severe attack of lumbago, but at the time he moved with the speed of a young man, shooting an arm round Paul's neck from behind, jerking his chin up and pulling him off balance, giving Felix a chance to dive for Paul's legs and pull his feet from under him. As he floundered on the floor, Nigel sat down heavily astride him, pinning his arms down, while Patrick, managing to look as if such scenes were normal occurrences in the drawing-rooms of his clients, went to telephone the police.

In the end it was not Felix's dramatics that convicted Paul, for when the police arrived he denied that his attack on Felix was to be taken as in any sense a confession. He had merely lost his temper, he said, at having such outrageous accusations made against him. But the police found traces of mud on his shoes which had not come from the drive and which

238

matched the mud in the lane at Deepstead, and there were splashes of mud too on the trousers that he had worn that day, which he had evidently tried to sponge off, but not too successfully. Felix, a little to his disappointment, was not even called to give evidence at the trial. He had seen himself as the perfect witness, lucid and helpful. However, without his assistance, the verdict was one of guilty.

Meg was very unhappy about it for a while and went to visit Paul in prison when it was possible, having apparently forgotten that Patrick had ever meant anything to her and transferred her affections to Paul. But I did not think that he would be the last love of her life. She took the job that Patrick had once offered her in the firm of Huddleston, Huddleston and Weekes, and found a bed-sitting-room in Allingford and I soon used to meet her here and there in the town in the company of the young sergeant who had helped Superintendent Chance to investigate the murders. The young man seemed to me a more stable type than either Patrick or Paul and probably better suited to her, but my faith in my own judgement of people had been badly damaged and I did not trust myself when it came to foretelling her future.

Felix stayed the night after Paul's arrest and we had a talk over more sandwiches and coffee.

'I don't know why you didn't tell me the truth about why Meg came to see you this afternoon,' I said. 'Why didn't you tell me it was about the mud on Paul's shoes and not about Patrick's destroying the will?'

'But I did tell you the truth,' he said. 'She only talked about Huddleston and the will.'

'Do you mean she didn't actually say anything about Paul's shoes?'

'Not a word. Didn't you notice she nearly contradicted me flatly when I said she had? Then she kept quiet out of curiosity. I was taking a bit of a risk, but I thought I could count on that. She wanted to know what I was leading up to.'

'I see. And about your alibi. The police aren't going to be too pleased with you for telling them that story about having spent the evening with the Lewises.'

'But I did spend it with the Lewises.'

'You didn't come down to Allingford with the Bodwells?'

'Certainly not.'

'Or hear Paul walking down the drive with them, imploring them not to tell anyone about having seen Imogen's murder, or Rita moan, or any of the things you said happened?'

'Good lord, no. You don't really think I'd have done nothing about it if I'd been there and seen it, do you? You don't think I'm as low as that. Though come to think of it . . .' He paused, stirring some sugar into his coffee.

240

'You may be quite right, I'd probably have been too scared of a man with a gun to show myself. But I think I'd have gone to the police straight away.'

'So your whole story was guesswork.'

'I don't like that word, guesswork,' he said. 'I prefer to call it an exercise of the imagination. I could see it all so clearly in my mind's eye, even how Paul got the gun and the reason he didn't kill Imogen with it. You see, I'm fairly sure he didn't know he was going to kill Imogen until he actually did it. I think she must have been a good deal to blame for driving him into a blind rage. Anyway, I think he did it impulsively. But when the Bodwells came in and demanded money, he had time to think and he said to them he'd go to his room and get what money he had, which he did, but he also went to the morning-room and got the gun, then he went with them to the car, and all the rest of it was just as I said.'

'I still call it guesswork.'

He shook his head. 'Perhaps if I'd been wrong I'd have agreed with you, but I was absolutely right, wasn't I?'

'That isn't the point.'

'You'd sooner have me prosaically accurate, but wrong, than imaginative and right?'

'I'm not sure that I wouldn't.'

He gave a sigh. 'It's a great pity, we'll never understand one another.'

'Well, that's the truth, anyway.'

'I'm so fond of you, you know.'

'I'm fond of you too.'

'Well, there we are then.'

'Yes, there we are.'

Soon afterwards we said good night and went upstairs to our rooms.

In the morning Felix brought me a cup of tea in bed, but when I went downstairs presently he had gone already, leaving a note for me on the kitchen table.

It said, 'I've taken five pounds from your handbag to see me home—I hope you don't mind. I'll send you a cheque tomorrow. Is there any reason why we shouldn't keep in touch occasionally? I've enjoyed seeing you. Let me know if you have another murder. I'm not sure I haven't found my métier. F.'

I got myself some breakfast. Then I went upstairs to make my bed and dismantle Felix's. In my bedroom I noticed the bottle of *Alliage* that he had brought me a few days before and suddenly I began to cry. I cried quietly for about an hour, I missed him so. At different times since I had known him I had loved him, hated him and for a while had even come near to tolerating him and that had been the most dangerous of all for me, because if ever I had settled down to putting up with him, I should entirely have lost myself. And I suppose that would have been a matter of some importance, though at times it is hard to be sure.

We hope you have enjoyed this Large Print book. Other Chivers Press or Thorndike Press Large Print books are available at your library or directly from the publishers.

For more information about current and forthcoming titles, please call or write, without obligation, to:

Chivers Large Print
published by BBC Audiobooks Ltd
St James House, The Square
Lower Bristol Road
Bath BA2 3SB
UK
email: bbcaudiobooks@bbc.co.uk
www.bbcaudiobooks.co.uk

OR

Thorndike Press
295 Kennedy Memorial Drive
Waterville
Maine 04901
USA
www.gale.com/thorndike
www.gale.com/wheeler

All our Large Print titles are designed for easy reading, and all our books are made to last.